'Yes.'

Mackenzie's lower lip began to wobble. 'Then things are *really* bad for my baby.'

'They're not good, Mackenzie.'

'And you...you'll just...help me? No questions asked? You'll just...help?' Her voice was choking with emotion and tears were beginning to gather behind her eyes. 'Just like that?'

John took both of her hands in his and gave them a little squeeze. 'Sometimes, Mackenzie, strangers are thrown together in difficult situations for no other reason than to offer comfort and support. I know what you're feeling.' He looked at their joined hands for a second before meeting her eyes once more. 'I lost my wife and daughter three years ago. I know what you're facing, and I desperately hope the outcome of your situation is far more positive than mine.'

'Oh, John.' Mackenzie blinked, unable to stop the tears from sliding down her cheeks. She was far too emotional, filled with all sorts of maternal hormones as well as with intense worry and concern for both Warick and her baby.

'That's all in the past.'

Although his words were soft, she could hear the gruff determination shining through.

'I'll help you through, Mackenzie. You can rely on me. No .... th that, he .... re they tur..........

Dear Reader

Sometimes there are books that flow beautifully...and others that take a little more coaxing. This story has definitely been the latter, but it's also become a labour of love. I've been attached to Mackenzie and John for quite some time, desperate to see them fall in love, but oftentimes the setting just wasn't quite right. Finally I feel they've found the most perfect home—managing to rely on each other in order to overcome the grief of their pasts and move forward into a bright and happy future, together with the gorgeous and effervescent Ruthie.

Overcoming grief is a long and drawn out process, sometimes taking many years before the sun can shine into your life once more. I am very saddened to say that while I was writing this story a young girl who was a dear friend to both our children suddenly passed away and we, as a family, found ourselves thrust into the world of grief that Mackenzie and John were also facing. Needless to say quite a few tears were shed during the creative and editing processes.

This story also marks the beginning of a new Lucy Clark series: *Sunshine General—Spreading a Little Sunshine*. At Sunshine General four close friends—Mackenzie, Bergan, Regina and Sunainah—will not only 'spread a little sunshine' but also meet four handsome doctors who will turn their well-ordered worlds upside down and inside out!

I hope you enjoy getting to know Mackenzie and John.

Warmest regards

Lucy

ONE
LIFE CHANGING
MOMENT

BY
LUCY CLARK

First published in Great Britain 2013
by Mills & Boon, an imprint of Harlequin (UK) Limited.
Harlequin (UK) Limited, Eton House,
18-24 Paradise Road, Richmond, Surrey TW9 1SR

© Anne Clark & Peter Clark 2013

ISBN: 978 0 263 89894 1

Harlequin (UK) policy is to use papers that are natural, renewable
and recyclable products and made from wood grown in sustainable
forests. The logging and manufacturing process conform to the
legal environmental regulations of the country of origin.

Printed and bound in Spain
by Blackprint CPI, Barcelona

Lucy Clark is actually a husband-and-wife writing team. They enjoy taking holidays with their children, during which they discuss and develop new ideas for their books using the fantastic Australian scenery. They use their daily walks to talk over characterisation and fine details of the wonderful stories they produce, and are avid movie buffs. They live on the edge of a popular wine district in South Australia with their two children, and enjoy spending family time together at weekends.

Recent titles by Lucy Clark:

DARE SHE DREAM OF FOREVER?
A SOCIALITE'S CHRISTMAS WISH
FALLING FOR DR FEARLESS
DIAMOND RING FOR THE ICE QUEEN
THE BOSS SHE CAN'T RESIST
WEDDING ON THE BABY WARD
SPECIAL CARE BABY MIRACLE

**These books are also available in eBook format
from www.millsandboon.co.uk**

For Zoe
Always smiling
Passionate about music
Lover of life
Beautiful princess
Rest peacefully
1999-2012
Rev 21:4

CHAPTER ONE

JOHN WATSON SMILED at something one of his adventure buddies had just said as the three men trudged their way through the scrub of Australia's Blue Mountains. They'd been up since six o'clock that morning, hiking out to a set of caves before exploring them. Dried mud and dirt was caked on his clothes, and his arm and leg muscles were pulsing with that satisfying pain that came after a good workout. They'd abseiled within the caves as well as doing a bit of climbing and he couldn't remember a more enjoyable day.

'Don't you think, John?' Stephen Brooks asked, and John lifted his head to look at his work colleague. John had only been working at Katoomba Hospital for the past six months and these weekend hikes had become something of a regular occurrence. He frowned for a moment, wondering if he wasn't becoming too attached, not only to the area but to the people he was working with. Keep your distance. That had been his mantra for the past three years.

'Sorry. I missed what you said.' John stopped walking and hitched up the large coil of rope presently slung over his shoulder. 'Would you look at that view?'

The other two men stopped and nodded. The sun was starting to dip lower in the sky, the reds, pinks and oranges of the approaching sunset starting to seep through the blue.

The gum-leaf green of the treetops spread before them, mixed with several shades of brown and yellow rock from the mountains added to the rich palette of colours. If any sight could be completely different from the views he'd grown up with as a boy in England, this was it.

'That's why you should accept the permanent job offer at the hospital,' Stephen added, shifting the equipment he carried to his opposite hand, the medical kit still firmly strapped to his back in a secure pack. 'You can rock-climb and cave and abseil to your heart's content.'

'It's a good perk,' Oliver, Stephen's brother-in-law, added. 'Good hospital, awesome people...' Oliver preened with a wide grin. 'Terrific adventures to be had and you're only two hours from Sydney for when you need a night on the town.'

'We'll even upgrade the tea-making facilities at the hospital. Get you your own pot and bone-china cup and saucer to appeal to your strong British sensibilities.'

'Now you're really sweetening the deal.' John laughed. It wasn't the first time Oliver and Stephen had tried to get him to accept the position of permanent orthopaedic surgeon at Katoomba Hospital but this time, after such a great day and now admiring the beauty surrounding him, he had to admit to being more tempted than before.

Their present serenity didn't last long, all three men snapping to attention when the sound of screeching tyres filled the air as a car, somewhere on the winding roads nearby, was clearly having difficulty staying on the road. The world seemed to stop spinning as the three of them held their breath, waiting, hoping against hope that the sickening crunch of crumpled automotive metal wouldn't be the next sound they heard. Their hope was unfounded and the horrific sound echoed off the mountains, magnifying its horror.

'Over there.' Oliver pointed in the direction of the road.

'Are you sure?' Stephen asked, but Oliver was already making a hasty new track through the scrub. John followed close behind, wondering just how long it would take the three of them to reach the accident site. As they hurried along, heading quickly down the small mountain they'd hiked up, conscious of their footing, a thousand different scenarios passed through his mind, effectively transferring his thoughts from the enjoyable day of adventure to the scenarios he knew went hand in hand with a motor vehicle accident.

All too soon they emerged from the scrub onto the road, not too far from where the sickening smell of burnt rubber, oil and the faint hint of petrol flooded the freshness of the surrounding forest. They sprinted down the bitumen towards a sedan that had careened off the road, bursting through the metal road barrier and meeting its end at the trunk of a thick and sturdy eucalyptus tree. They left their equipment off to the side but Stephen brought the medical bag with him.

Stephen already had his cellphone out, pleased there was reception in this section of the mountains, and was calling for an ambulance and emergency crews. Oliver and Stephen headed for the driver's side so John rounded the car to check the passenger side, astonished to find the door flung wide open. He quickly scanned the area, looking at the leaf-covered ground to see if he could identify a trail where the passenger may have gone. Yes.

'We've got a passenger who's managed to get out,' he told his colleagues.

'This guy is well and truly trapped,' Oliver said. 'Legs are crushed, seat belt has held him firm but we'll need to cut the steering column to get him out.'

'Can anyone else smell petrol?' Stephen asked.

'I can smell it,' John remarked, his senses heightening as he carefully followed the trail. He was peripherally aware of Stephen and Oliver, discussing tactics for quickly evacuating the driver in the case of a car fire. Stephen had grabbed the rope they'd used for rock climbing and Oliver was coming round to the passenger side in order to do a thorough evaluation on the driver who, from John's brief glimpse, was indeed in a bad way. All three men were part of the Blue Mountains retrieval teams so knew the protocols and procedures by heart.

'Hello?' John called as he walked away from the wreckage. 'Can you hear me? Anyone out here?'

His answer was a loud guttural yell, far too high-pitched to have come from a male. He quickly altered his course to head in the direction of the sound. 'Hello? I want to help you,' he said.

'Over…here.' The feminine voice panted, and concern ripped through him as he finally spotted the passenger. She had long blonde hair, half covering her face in a messy tangle, and was wearing a long blue dress, now rucked up to reveal her smooth legs. She was sitting down, her back against a tree for support, her knees bent up, and somewhere along the way she'd lost one of her flat satin shoes. And she was pregnant.

John rushed to her side. 'How many weeks are you?'

'Thirty-one.'

'And you're having contractions?'

She fixed him with a glare from a pair of gorgeous green eyes. 'I thought the yell and the way I'm desperately trying to control my breathing might have given you a clue, Brit boy.'

John couldn't help the small smile that twitched at the corners of his lips. 'I'm John, by the way. I'm a doctor. Do you mind if I…?' He pointed to her swollen belly.

'Be my guest, Dr John.' She took his hand in hers and guided it to her belly, where he could instantly feel the tightness.

'How many contractions have you had?'

'Five.'

'How far apart?' He gestured to the gold watch on her wrist. 'Have you been able to time them?'

'Three minutes apart. They're intense and I've already had the urge to push. If you have any sort of medical kit and just happen to be carrying an IV bag of salbutamol, that would be a great help.'

John raised his eyebrows at this. 'How many children have you had?' She certainly knew a lot about what was going on.

'This is my first.'

'You're a nurse? Midwife?'

'Try doctor.'

'You're a doctor?'

'Don't sound so surprised, Dr John. Women have been practising medicine for quite some time now.'

John continued to feel her abdomen as well as checking her ankles for swelling. 'No sign of pre-eclampsia. Were you having contractions before the crash?' He took her wrist in his and counted the beats.

'I had Braxton-Hicks' but that's normal and, besides, I still have at least six weeks to go so I didn't think anything of it.'

She continued to focus on her breathing, keeping it nice and steady, relaxing as much as she could in the circumstances.

'I need to go get a few things from the medical kit,' John remarked, but as he stood up the woman reached for his hand, holding it tightly in hers. She looked into his eyes and he instantly saw her fear and concern.

'My…my husband?' She shook her head. 'I looked at him after the crash and the sight made me feel ill—so I got out. I just had to. Is he…?' She left the sentence hanging.

'My colleagues are with him. They're trained and experienced doctors and they're doing everything they can to help him.'

She seemed to relax at this news, leaning her head back against the tree and closing her eyes, but she still held firm to John's hand.

'What's your name?' he asked softly as he knelt down.

'Mackenzie.' As she spoke the word, she clenched her teeth. 'Looks like our three minutes of chatting time is up, Dr John.' And she gripped his hand tighter as the next contraction seized her. She panted, doing her best to control the pain, channelling all her tension into his hand, but John didn't mind. In the middle of the contraction, though, she gave another guttural yell and even through the blue material of her dress he could see the tension in her belly.

'That's a push,' he murmured, more to himself than to her, but Mackenzie opened her eyes and glared at him as the contraction began to subside.

'I know it's a push,' she growled. 'I felt it.' She sighed and leaned her head back against the tree. 'But I couldn't control it.' She whimpered a little as though she was already too tired to continue.

John heard the devastation in her words because they both clearly recognised the difficulty of their present predicament. The birth of a premature baby was problematic enough when surrounded by the best medical equipment in the world, but out here, in the scrub lands, in the middle of nowhere…

'Let me get the medical kit. I don't think we have IV salbutamol but there's definitely an inhaler, although I don't think that's going to help much. Do you have any heart conditions? Respiratory problems?'

'No and no. Go, get the medical kit.' Mackenzie opened her eyes and looked up at him, calling to him as he turned to walk away. 'And, er…John…can you let me know how Warick's doing?'

He nodded. 'Of course.'

'We were arguing.' The words seemed to rush from her lips, her voice wavering, and when she raised a hand to her mouth he noticed it was shaking. 'He wanted me to go with him to his business dinner but I didn't want to go. I didn't feel well but he insisted it would look silly if he turned up without his wife as all the other wives would be there and so I acquiesced and we set off but he was still mad and then he was taking the turns too fast and…and…'

Tears started to slide slowly down her cheeks and John instantly knelt down beside her once more, taking her trembling hand in his.

'Shh. It wasn't your fault.'

'But I was yelling at him. Telling him that I didn't feel well and that…that…if he didn't slow down he'd kill us both.' Mackenzie broke down and started to cry. John instantly gathered her close into his arms and held her as she sobbed. 'He's…in…such a…bad way,' she hiccuped between sobs. 'I couldn't…help him. I…had to get…out of the…'

'You were thinking about the baby. That's a natural maternal instinct.' Her sobs were starting to subside but were replaced with yet another contraction. John had one arm around her shoulder, the other holding her hand, or rather allowing his hand to be pulverised into a purplish colour by Mackenzie.

When it was over, she sagged against him, snuggling momentarily into the warmth of his broad and powerful shoulders, unable to believe how incredible it felt just to be held, to be cared for.

There were times when she wanted nothing more than to simply be held, to be told everything would be all right. Throughout her life, thanks to her parents' selfishness, she'd been integrated into the New South Wales foster system from the age of ten, which meant Mackenzie hadn't had too many opportunities to rely on other people.

'They'll always let you down,' Bergan, one of her foster-sisters, had told her. 'Be strong. Stand on your own two feet. Don't trust anyone.'

They had been powerful words to Mackenzie and it had taken years for her to realise that at times she *needed* to trust others, that she simply couldn't make it through her life all on her own.

In medical school she'd found a group of women, all very different from her but somehow all of them had bonded in a friendship that had lasted decades. Then, when she'd been working day and night as an intern, she'd met Warick and she'd taken a huge chance and given in to his constant pleas for her to marry him.

Now Warick was trapped in a car, fighting for his life, while she was about to bring another life into this crazy, mixed-up world. She'd escaped from the confines of the car and, after smelling petrol in the air, had made her way to a safe distance. The contractions had forced a plethora of scenarios to flood through her mind, the worst being that she would give birth to a thirty-one-week gestation baby who wouldn't survive long in this world without medical care.

Then she'd heard male voices and John had appeared. Big, strong, John who was holding her as though she was incredibly important to him. John, who was going to help her while his friends helped Warick. She hadn't needed to ask whether they'd called for back-up because she, too, knew emergency protocols. Help was on the way. She just had to hold on…and John was with her. Helping her. Comforting her. Supporting her.

'I'll go and get the medical supplies.' His words were soft and gentle near her ear and he slowly eased her from his strong hold. He looked into her eyes, the fading light still allowing her to see his sincerity. 'I won't be long.' He tenderly placed her head against the tree. 'Just rest and relax. I'll be back before you know it.' His smile was warm and encouraging and filled with a promise she somehow knew he wouldn't break.

'OK.' Mackenzie breathed, accepting the smile he aimed in her direction. Through drowsy eyes she watched him walk away from her, instantly wishing him back. At some point he'd become her strength and right now, given her present predicament, she knew she needed to rely on his borrowed strength to see her through.

She had no idea who John was, whether he was married with a family of his own. She knew he was a doctor with a brilliant bedside manner and a gorgeous smile. In such a short space of time she'd not only come to rely on him, she'd come to trust him.

CHAPTER TWO

'RIGHT. I THINK we're ready to begin.' Mackenzie walked into the operating room, gowned and gloved and ready for the next patient. 'We have Mrs Neve Windslow, who requires an open reduction and internal fixation of her left tibia.' She glanced around the operating room at the staff. 'I know it's been a long night in Theatre and you're all tired but this is the last patient on the list so focus, people. Let's get the job done.'

It was quite common when there was a multiple pile-up on the motorway for all of Sunshine General Hospital's five emergency theatres to be going all night and all day. Mackenzie had been rostered on-call this evening and now, as the clock ticked around to five o'clock in the morning, they were thankfully in the final stages of applying the external fixator to Mrs Windslow's shin bone.

Mackenzie could feel the ache in her shoulders, the one she'd spent the better part of her shift ignoring, begin to make itself known. Soon. Soon she would be finished then she could check on her patients and go and collect her daughter. Ruthie's cuddles always managed to ease the pressure of Mackenzie's hectic work schedule.

There were several people in Theatre, some she knew and worked with on a regular basis and some she'd never seen before, given the hectic emergency operating schedule. Even though everyone was gowned, gloved and wearing theatre masks and shields, she knew who most of the regular staff were simply by looking at their eyes.

Theatre sister Anna had very light blue eyes; the anaesthetist, Pavlov, had green with a swirl of yellow; her orthopaedic registrar, Sonny, had dark brown eyes that sometimes looked almost black. Right now, though, it didn't matter who was handing her instruments or who was swabbing the patient's leg or who was assisting her to attach the final part of the metal fixator because once the job was done, they'd all be able to finally go home.

'Excuse me,' the scout nurse said, phone in her hand. 'I have a message for Sonny.' She looked at the orthopaedic registrar, who was concentrating on tightening the metal screw into place.

'Can you take a message?' Mackenzie asked.

'Uh…it's his wife. She's just been admitted to the maternity ward. Her labour is progressing rapidly.'

'What?' Sonny almost dropped the screwdriver. Mackenzie reached over and took it out of his hand, passing it to Anna.

'Go,' she stated.

'But we're almost done here and—'

'You're about to become a father and, believe me, you won't want to miss a second of the whole event.'

Images of Ruthie's entrance into the world flashed through her mind. It had been the worst night of Mackenzie's life, except for John Watson. Her knight in shining armour. John had been the one to deliver Ruthie and also the one to inform her of Warick's death. One life lost, one life gained.

She gave herself a mental shake. After Bergan had arrived at the Sydney children's hospital to support her, John Watson had gone back to where he'd come from. She hadn't heard from him again in five years and while at times she'd wondered what might have happened to him, no one really wanted to be reminded of the worst night of their life, especially not her. She was a survivor and, as such, she'd locked that night up tight and pushed it into the 'Do not open' section of her mind.

'We'll be fine here,' Mackenzie stated, her words coming out more briskly than she'd intended. She glanced at Sonny and saw he was still in two minds whether or not to go. 'Go…Sonny. Oh, and don't forget to text me. I want to know all the details.'

Several other people agreed as Sonny headed out of the theatre; others called their best wishes.

Mackenzie sighed and looked down at Mrs Windslow's leg. So close to finishing and one step closer to having Ruthie's little arms about her neck, hugging her close. The world kept on turning. With that sobering thought she snapped her mind back into theatre mode and glanced quickly around the room.

'Right. Can someone please come and hold this last section of the fixator so I can screw it into place?'

'I'll help,' a deep, rich voice replied, and a shiver shimmied its way down Mackenzie's spine. It sounded very like a voice she'd heard before. A voice she knew she'd never forget, but it couldn't possibly be…

Her mouth went dry and her entire body froze, a wave of confusion and piercing pain washing over her as she ever so slowly raised her gaze to the person now standing opposite her. A gowned and gloved figure with hypnotic blue eyes shielded by the surgical mask.

'Mackenzie?' Anna asked, holding the screwdriver out towards her.

Mackenzie didn't hear anything, the vague sounds of the operating theatre fading into oblivion as she continued to stare into those bluest of blue eyes. They were eyes she would never forget. The smell of dried leaves, of sweat, of pain and of petrol filled her nostrils as a barrage of images flooded her mind, the images she could have sworn she'd locked safely away.

Arguing with Warick. Asking him to slow down. Her hand on the dashboard of the car as she adjusted the seat belt around her pregnant belly. The sickening sound of crushed metal. The sight of Warick's body bruised and bloodied, almost melded into the car. The pain in her abdomen. The tightening. The rush of nausea forcing her fumbling hands to unbuckle the belt, to open the door, to escape the confines of the car. The realisation she was in labour. That she would give birth. That she'd be all alone...again.

'Mackenzie?' Anna called, but her voice sounded muffled and far away. Mackenzie tried to swallow but found her mouth dry as she stared into the eyes of the man standing across the operating table.

'John?' The whispered word was wrenched from her dry throat. One terrible memory after another began swamping her mind and she felt her knees start to buckle, her head pounding with repressed anguish.

She reached out blindly towards someone near her but missed, unable to focus clearly. The last thing she remembered was falling forward and hearing a deep voice call out, 'Catch her,' before darkness overcame her.

With one last, almighty push, combined with another guttural yell, Mackenzie collapsed back against the ambulance stretcher and waited.

'It's a girl,' John announced as he and the paramedic set about suctioning out the baby's lungs, rubbing her vigorously, doing anything and everything they could to keep the tiny little girl alive until they reached the hospital. John had been hoping amongst hope that Mackenzie would be able to wait but her impatient daughter had clearly had other ideas. 'How far are we?' he asked.

'Approximately two minutes out,' the paramedic replied.

'Tell me what's going on,' Mackenzie demanded. 'I want to know.'

The paramedic met John's gaze and softly shook his head but even though John had only known Mackenzie for such a short space of time, he'd already realised she was a strong woman. Plus, as she was a doctor, he knew her mind was no doubt racing with different scenarios and the best way to stop her wondering was to do as she'd asked.

'We're trying to get her breathing. Initial Apgar is four. She's small but complete.' John continued to use the suction to remove the mucus from the baby's mouth and nose. 'Organise oxygen saturations via non-rebreather child mask.' John had wrapped the baby in a towel and was gently rubbing her skin to stimulate circulation while he hooked a stethoscope into his ears. He listened to her breathing.

'Lungs have fluid. There's a heart murmur.' He lifted his head and stared at the paramedic. 'You've radioed for a humidi-crib and paediatric consul—'

'Greg's responded. He's waiting for us.'

'Excellent.'

'Who's Greg?'

'Paediatric consultant. We used to work together at Sydney's children's hospital years ago. He's very qualified and very good.' John hoped his tone was reassuring because from the look of Mackenzie's little girl she was going to need every ounce of Greg's expertise.

The ambulance began to slow down as the driver navigated the vehicle into the hospital grounds. Within the next moment, the two external doors were opened and Mackenzie's sick little girl was handed off to people she'd never met before.

'John? John?' Mackenzie called. 'What's happening?'

He was back by her side, pulling off his gloves and putting them into the rubbish bin. 'She's with Greg and his team. They're putting her into the humidi-crib. Come on, let's get you out of this confined space and off to the maternity ward.'

'I'm fine. I can walk,' she said, and tried to get off the bed.

'Where do you think you're going?' John demanded, placing a gentle hand on her shoulder. 'I may be an orthopaedic surgeon who's not used to delivering babies but I *do* know that you should lie there and not be so stubborn.' He looked into her eyes, holding her gaze. 'I'll wheel you to Maternity myself and I'll help you in any way I can.'

John's tone held the promise of his words and Mackenzie knew he meant it. She reached for his hand, which he immediately offered, and with a gentle, reassuring squeeze she felt her immediate panic and fear begin to subside. She rested back against the stretcher and closed her eyes.

'We're good to go,' she heard him tell the paramedic and, true to his word, all too soon she was up in the maternity suite. John gathered intel on her daughter's condition while the nurses helped her to have a quick shower, her lovely blue dress which Warick had bought her during the first year of their marriage now ruined. Afterwards, dressed in a hospital gown, she allowed the nurses to take her observations, pleased with her results.

She was about to get out of bed again and go and see what was happening with her baby girl when John walked back into her room.

'Well?'

'She's breathing but she's not doing too well.'

'Can I see her?'

'Absolutely.' He came round to the side of the bed, picking up the hospital robe and holding it out to her. 'Have you thought about any names?'

'Yes, but Warick and I couldn't agree.'

'Which names did you like?'

'I liked Ruthie for a girl. I once had a foster-sister called Ruthie but Warick didn't like it.'

'Did you know you were having a girl?'

'No. I wanted to keep the gender of the baby a surprise. Warick was determined it would be a boy and so he picked only boys' names.' Although she wanted to rush, Mackenzie forced herself to take her time, having been astounded at how exhausted she'd felt after just having a shower. 'Is there any news on—?'

'I haven't heard but I will tell you the instant I do.' Again, there was that deep promise in his tone, as though he would never try to hide anything from her. He held out his hand. 'Let's go and see your daughter.'

As they walked down the corridor to the nursery, Mackenzie held firmly to John's hand. 'Is it bad?'

'Greg's recommending surgery. The hole in her heart isn't showing signs of closing.'

Mackenzie processed this information. 'She'll need to be transferred.'

'Greg's on the phone to Sydney children's hospital right now.'

'I'm going with her.'

'Of course.'

She looked up at him as they continued their slow but steady progress to the nursery. 'You won't try and stop me?'

'Your observations are fine. You're a doctor. You know

the protocols but, above all, she's your daughter.' His blue eyes pierced her own. 'You need to be with her.'

Before this night was out Mackenzie ran the risk of losing not only her husband but possibly her daughter as well. John's heart ached for her. He knew exactly how she must be feeling and he wanted to do everything he could to help her through this.

'But Warick?'

'As I said, we'll be kept informed.'

'We?' She'd stopped just outside the nursery and stared into his eyes. 'Are you planning to come to Sydney with me?'

'Yes.'

Mackenzie's lower lip began to wobble. 'Then things are *really* bad for my baby.'

'They're not good, Mackenzie.'

'And you…you'll just…help me? No questions asked? You'll just…help?' Her voice was choking over with emotion and tears were beginning to gather behind her eyes. 'Just like that?'

John took both of her hands in his and gave them a little squeeze. 'Sometimes, Mackenzie, strangers are thrown together in difficult situations for no other reason than to offer comfort and support. I know what you're feeling.' He looked at their joined hands for a second before meeting her eyes once more.

'Oh, John.' Mackenzie blinked, unable to stop the tears from sliding down her cheeks. She was far too emotional, filled with all sorts of maternal hormones as well as intense worry and concern for both Warick and her baby.

'I'll help you through this, Mackenzie. You can rely on me.' Although his words were soft, she could hear the gruff determination shining through. 'Now, let's go see your beautiful Ruthie.' With that, he gave her hands another little squeeze before they turned and entered the nursery.

'Mackenzie?'

'John?' she called weakly.

'I'm here. It's OK.' His British tones came softly near her ear and Mackenzie started to relax a little. 'You're OK,' he reiterated and she managed to breathe out slowly. His voice was so close, so vibrant and so real. She'd often thought about his lovely voice over the years, of the way he'd been her rock in her most desperate time of trouble and how she'd never really had the opportunity to thank him properly.

'John?' she murmured again, as thoughts and images flooded her mind. Where was she? What was happening? She strained hard to think. She wasn't leaning against a tree, gritting her teeth against contractions.

She wasn't in hospital as a patient, she was in hospital as a doctor. She was a trained orthopaedic surgeon at Sunshine General Hospital in Queensland and she'd been operating in Theatre all night long. She'd been almost finished with her final patient, Mrs Windslow, and then…and then Sonny had been called away and…and…she'd looked across the table and…

Mackenzie's heart pounded against her ribs and her eyes snapped open. She sat bolt upright, almost head-butting John in the process. 'John?' His name was a disbelieving whisper, her eyes as wide as saucers.

'Hello.' He was crouched on one knee beside her, smiling brightly.

'Wh-what happened? Where am I?' She looked around, realising she was in the anteroom outside the operating theatre, lying on the floor. She was still dressed in her bloodied theatre gown, although someone had removed her gloves, shield and mask.

'You fainted,' he supplied, answering her first question.

'Why…? How…? Why are you here?' She continued to stare at him as he stood up and stepped back. Anna bustled into the area and quickly knelt down beside Mackenzie.

'I was so worried. What on earth happened? I've never known you to faint before. You're not pregnant again, are you?' Anna chattered like a mother hen caring for one of her chicks as she untied Mackenzie's theatre gown.

At the word 'pregnant', she glanced at John and saw him raise an eyebrow. She ignored Anna's questions. 'The patient? Mrs Windslow?'

'I finished the surgery,' John remarked. 'She's off in Recovery and doing fine.'

'How long was I out?' Mackenzie asked as she started scrambling to her feet, her theatre gumboots not giving her the traction she needed in order to stand. John instantly placed a hand beneath her elbow to assist her, causing warmth and a plethora of tingles to shoot right through her entire body at the simple touch.

As soon as she was upright, she jerked away from him, doing her best to ignore the increased pounding of her heart against her chest. One brief touch from him and she was a mass of nerves and excitement. Why? Was it embarrassment? The uncertainty of how to behave around the man who had seen her through her darkest hours? Who'd witnessed all the vulnerabilities she'd spent a lifetime learning to hide from others?

'About fifteen minutes,' Anna fussed. 'Not like you at all but, then again, it has been rather an arduous night and no doubt you've probably not eaten much.' The theatre nurse tsked, as she continued to help Mackenzie completely degown, removing the big rubber boots from her feet and offering the clogs that Mackenzie had left in the anteroom so many long hours ago.

'I think a cup of tea's in order,' John remarked. 'Very British, I know, but we do believe that a nice cup of tea can set things to rights again.'

'Nice sweet tea,' Anna said approvingly as she stared at Mackenzie with concern. 'She does still look a bit peaky. Yes, take her away to the cafeteria and get some sugar into her, Dr er... What did you say your name was?'

'Watson,' he supplied, unable to drag his gaze away from Mackenzie. She was clearly confused as to his presence and he was silently berating himself for not announcing his presence properly when he'd entered her theatre, but, then again, he hadn't expected her to faint. She was the strongest woman he'd ever known and so the possibility of her passing out hadn't even entered his thoughts.

Not only did he really want a cup of tea, especially after the night the entire theatre department had just endured, he also wanted to give Mackenzie the opportunity to ask him whatever questions were currently churning around in that intelligent mind of hers.

Deciding it would also be best not to touch her any more, given that simply helping her to her feet had caused his gut to tighten, a sensation he certainly hadn't experienced the last time he'd been with Mackenzie Fawles, John stepped back and swept his open hand towards the door. 'Shall we?'

Mackenzie was still giving him quizzical looks but when Anna shooed her out the door, she did as she was told. As the two of them walked out of Theatre and into the main corridor, John remained silent, allowing Mackenzie to lead the way both in the course of the conversation and also in their present direction.

'This way,' she murmured as they came to a T-junction

of corridors. That was all she said and as she was walking rather fast, he was having difficulty getting a good read on her expression. Finally she asked, 'Is this your first visit to Sunshine General?'

'I'm here to spread a little sunshine,' he quipped, but Mackenzie didn't even smile.

'That's the oldest joke here, John,' she pointed out as they walked into the crowded cafeteria. 'I'll even go so far as to advise you not to try it out on anyone else.'

'Advice accepted,' he murmured with mock contriteness. He followed her to a self-serve tea and coffee bar, the scent of bacon and eggs filling the air as hospital personnel tucked into a hearty breakfast, a lot of them still dressed in scrubs, like Mackenzie and himself. It had indeed been a long night in Theatre for a lot of people. He may have come to Sunshine General in an official capacity but when he'd seen Mackenzie's name on the list of orthopaedic consultants, his mind had been assailed with a barrage of memories.

He'd often thought about her over the years, wondering how her life had turned out. He'd helped her face some terrible situations and in turn it had caused his own repressed memories of love and loss to rise to the surface. In the end, once he'd known she was going to be all right, he'd quietly taken his leave and slipped out of her life as easily as he'd slipped into it.

'This isn't tea,' he complained after jiggling a teabag up and down in a plastic cup.

Mackenzie smiled. 'You're so British, John.'

He stared at her, looking at the light in her eyes as her lips curved upwards. She was beautiful. There was no doubt about it. Even though her blonde hair was pulled back into a ponytail, he could tell it was shorter than last time he'd seen her. She had a few more laughter lines around her dazzling green eyes, which made him glad. During their short acquaintance all those years ago she certainly hadn't had anything to smile about but now, as he watched her sit amongst the hustle and bustle of a busy hospital, smiling so naturally at *him*, it caused his gut to tighten.

Did Mackenzie feel that same strange undercurrent presently passing between the two of them? Had she pulled away from him in the anteroom because she'd been affected by his nearness or repulsed by it? Did she loathe him, connecting his face with the horrific memories of her past? Or was there something more, something…new?

The smile was beginning to fade from her lips and it was only then he realised he was staring. He quickly looked down at his tea, wanting desperately to put her at ease once more, to see her smile return.

'How long have you been working here at Sunshine General?' he tried in an attempt at normal conversation, even though he'd already read her personnel file.

'I moved here once Ruthie had been discharged from the children's hospital in Sydney.' Mackenzie sighed and looked down into her cup, not really seeing anything but the past. 'After…everything, well, I needed a complete change of scene, a fresh start, and I had friends here.'

'You had a friend in Sydney, too. Bergan, wasn't it?'

'That's right.' She forced herself to look at him, to meet his eyes—eyes that had seen her at her most vulnerable. Hopefully now, when he looked at her, he'd see a different woman, one who was more in control of her life than the mess she'd been back then.

'Bergan was also moving from Sydney to here and there was a job opening in Orthopaedics so it seemed like the right thing to do. When you don't have any family of your own, you tend to build one as best you can.'

'Sometimes those are the better families,' John remarked gently.

Mackenzie took a big gulp of her tea, not really tasting it. 'Well, after growing up in various foster-homes, pulling a family together from those I've learned to trust is the only way to go.'

'Do you trust me?' The question came from his lips before he could stop it and his answer was one haughtily raised eyebrow from Mackenzie.

'To a point.'

His smile was instant. 'You haven't changed a bit. Still so forthright. I like it.'

'Blunt,' she offered, the eyebrow lowering and her lips twitching slightly. 'Call a spade a spade, John.'

'I do but there's no harm in employing a touch of diplomacy either,' he offered, and took a sip of his tea, pulling a face afterwards. 'This really is quite ghastly. How anyone can call this tea is beyond me.'

Mackenzie's answer was to finish off her tea, crush the cup and lob it neatly into the nearest bin.

'Good shot.'

'Thanks, tea snob.'

'I *am*. I freely admit it. At the last hospital I worked at I ended up bringing in my own teapot, filtered water and selection of teas.'

She smiled at his words as he reluctantly took another sip of the drink, once more pulling a face. 'Which hospital was that?'

'Adelaide General.'

'Well, everyone knows the water isn't the best in Adelaide. If it's good water you're after, Canberra's water supply is good and it's not too bad—'

'Are you really going to sit there and give me a breakdown of the different types of tap water in this country?'

Mackenzie levelled him with a look. 'You're the one who was complaining about the tea.' There was a hint of annoyance in her tone and she wished she could have stopped it. A range of different emotions passed through her, ranging from curiosity to embarrassment. How was she supposed to act when the man sitting opposite her, complaining about tea, was the same man who had helped her through one of the most difficult times in her life? For almost forty-eight hours John Watson had stayed by her side, helping her, guiding her, listening to her, holding her, when she'd been unable to remain strong with wave after wave of tears pouring down her face.

And then…as if by magic, he'd disappeared. Bergan had arrived on the scene to help Mackenzie and with that John had gone, leaving a note with the nursing staff, stating he was returning to Katoomba and that he wished her and Ruthie all the best.

John eased back in his chair, watching her with interest. 'You're mad at me.'

'No. Not mad. Surprised to see you, here, at my hospital. Which naturally begs the question—what *are* you doing at Sunshine General? And, more specifically, what were you doing in *my* theatre?'

'I thought that might have been obvious. Half the theatre staff had been working round the clock, all night long, and reinforcements were called in to help.'

'You were one of the reinforcements?'

'I'd not long finished in theatre five, heard you were just finishing up and thought I'd look in to see if there was anything I could do. Turned out there was.'

'So you're working here now, is that it?' John's answer was to finish the rest of his foul tea. 'First the Blue Mountains, then Adelaide, now here. You sure get around, Dr Watson.'

'Actually, after the Blue Mountains I headed back to England for a year then started working my way around three different counties, helping out here and there. Then to the United States for six months then Tarparnii and then finally back to Australia where, yes, I worked in Melbourne then Adelaide and now here.'

'You really *do* get around. Why is that?'

He shrugged. 'I like to meet people.'

'Or you're lonely.' She held his gaze.

'There you go again. Calling a spade a spade.'

'I'm right, though.'

John shrugged one shoulder. 'The Sunshine Coast has wonderful winter weather. Much the same as an English summer. What's not to like?'

'You've come here for the weather?'

'That and the fact that they offered me the position of Director of Orthopaedics, at least for the next twelve months.'

Mackenzie couldn't stop her jaw from growing slack at this news. 'You're the new director?'

He grinned, scrunched his paper cup with delight then followed her lead and lobbed it neatly into the bin before winking at her. 'I'm your new boss.'

CHAPTER THREE

ANNA HAD BEEN well pleased with the colour in Mackenzie's face when they'd met in the female change rooms later.

'Much better.' Anna patted Mackenzie's cheeks then leaned back to study her with an air of mischief. 'But I need to know…is the colour in your cheeks from having sweetened tea or the handsome man who sat opposite you?' Anna giggled and fanned her face with her hand. 'That man is gorgeous.'

'And you're a married woman,' Mackenzie replied, not wanting to talk about John. Of course, there was no denying his good looks. It was a fact, pure and simple. The *other* fact, the one she was more than willing to refute, was that one simple look from John Watson could spin her heart into a possible myocardial infarction. That had never happened before and she didn't even want to think about what it might possibly mean.

She'd thought about him a lot over the years, of the way he'd helped her, listened to her, believed in her even when she hadn't believed in herself. She knew next to nothing about his personal life other than he was British, and most people could tell that from his accent.

Now, five years later, Mackenzie still had no idea whether he was married or had children. While he seemed able to draw information out of her, he was extremely guarded when it came to offering something back. What was it that made John Watson tick? Mackenzie wished she didn't care but even now the mere mention of his name was enough to spark her interest.

'Hey, no harm in looking.' Anna waggled her eyebrows up and down. 'And while I may be married, you are most definitely not.'

'I don't need another husband, Anna. Losing one was more than enough for me to bear.'

'You've been a widow for over five years now.'

Mackenzie nodded as she finished changing. 'I'm well aware of that fact.'

'You don't deserve to spend the rest of your life alone,' Anna implored, reaching out to cup a handful of Mackenzie's blonde hair. 'You're so pretty and you've been through so much. You deserve happiness.'

Mackenzie chuckled. 'Well, if happiness is your agenda, don't start by wishing me another husband. Ruthie and I are fine by ourselves. We've made do over the years, building our own little family here at the hospital. I simply don't have room for any new people in my life right now.' She picked up her light jacket, perfect for the July winter weather in Queensland, and closed her locker door. She looked at Anna, then stepped forward and gave the other woman a hug.

'Thanks for your concern, though. I do appreciate it.' Mackenzie buckled her watch to her wrist and checked the time. It was a quarter to six. 'I've got to go. By the time I've finished doing a quick round of Recovery and ICU, I'll get a full hour with Ruthie before I need to get her ready for school.'

'Give her a kiss from me. We all love little Ruthie.'

Mackenzie smiled, pleased she'd managed to change the topic of conversation from the discombobulating John

Watson to her gorgeous daughter. 'Will do.' She picked up her bag and started for the door, calling goodbye to Anna as she went out.

In Recovery, she headed to the nurses' station to review Mrs Windslow's progress and was surprised to find John standing there, reading another patient's notes. He was also standing directly in front of the filing cabinet containing her patient's information. He didn't look up from what he was reading, didn't even seem aware of her presence. Mackenzie cleared her throat impatiently.

'Excuse me, Dr Watson. Would you mind passing me Mrs Windslow's casenotes, please?'

John looked up from what he was reading, seemingly astonished to find her there. 'Mackenzie! Sorry.' He quickly shifted out of the way, collected Mrs Windslow's casenotes and handed them to her with one his heart-melting smiles. 'Here you go.'

'Thank you.' They stood side by side at the nurses' station, reading and making notations on the notes, as the rest of the recovery staff rushed around, caring for their plethora of patients. Mackenzie felt strange. She had no idea why she was so aware of him, why every single move he made, even if it was just to shuffle his feet, sparked off an alarm deep within her.

When he'd been with her before, he'd been her rock, the man she could lean on, who understood what it was like to lose a spouse. He'd been kind, caring, giving and thoughtful and even though she'd recognised he was everything Warick hadn't been, she still hadn't experienced anything like the deep sensual awareness she felt now.

Add to that disturbing fact the knowledge that John Watson was her new boss and Mackenzie was starting to realise that she might be venturing into uncharted territory. Being attracted to one's boss wasn't a good thing and it simply meant she'd have to work extra hard in order to find some level of neutrality so she didn't feel as uncomfortable as she did right now.

After he'd revealed his new position of authority, Mackenzie had started to feel her world begin to spin a little unevenly. John hadn't only appeared in her theatre, reviving memories she'd thought locked away for ever, he was here to stay, at least for the next twelve months. Drawing in a slow, deep breath, she'd nodded politely and offered what she'd hoped sounded like positive and sincere congratulations before rising from her chair.

She'd been more surprised when John had followed suit, easily falling into step with her as they'd made their way out of the cafeteria, heading down the long corridor back towards the emergency theatre block changing rooms.

'You don't have to walk with me,' she'd said. 'I know the way.'

'I don't. This place is more of a rabbit warren than other hospitals I've been in.'

'I think you're lying.'

He'd shrugged one shoulder. 'Perhaps. Look, Mackenzie, I didn't mean my words just now to sound as though I was gloating. I wasn't. I was offered the job of director and I accepted. It really is as simple as that.'

'Of course.'

'And yet you still sound as though you don't believe me.' She hadn't ventured a reply and they'd continued to walk in silence for a minute before he'd said, 'Why didn't you apply for the job as director? You know the staff. You have the qualifications—'

'Wait.' She'd stopped momentarily and stared at him. 'How do you know what qualifications I have?' she'd asked.

'I've read your file. I've read everyone's file in the department but I have to say, yours is quite amazing. It's impressive that you started your Ph.D. during your registrar training. That's a fairly extensive workload.'

'And I finished it while I was working part time at a private practice, as well as juggling full-time sole parenting.' She'd shaken her head and started walking again. 'Men. You all seem to have a block when it comes to children. For a man, the career always comes first, yet for most women, children and family come first.'

She'd stopped again and pointed her finger at him. 'It's far harder for a woman to become a director or get accepted onto registrar training programmes or climb any sort of corporate ladder if she's putting her family first.'

'Agreed. I have four sisters, Mackenzie. They're all older than me and when our parents died when I was eight, the four of them raised me. They're all very different, very protective and very forthright, and I'm right behind all of them when it comes to advocating equal rights for women, hence why I mentioned that you most certainly had the qualifications for the job. The fact that you have chosen to put Ruthie first is not only the department's loss but Ruthie's gain.'

Mackenzie frowned and, realising he'd effectively taken the wind out of her sails by agreeing with her, she turned on her heel and started to walk again, not surprised when John easily fell into step beside her once more.

'Besides,' she muttered, 'I have a difficult enough time juggling my day-to-day workload, especially when I'm the surgeon on call, with Ruthie's routine, let alone the extra pressure of more meetings, more paperwork and far more responsibility than I want.'

'What about hiring a nanny? Surely you have someone to—?'

Mackenzie stopped short yet again and levelled a dan-

gerous stare at him. 'Look, John. You may have helped
me out years ago, you may have delivered my daughter
into this world, but don't for a moment think that gives
you any right to tell me how to live my life. I *choose* to
spend as much time with my daughter as possible. I've had
to make many sacrifices along the way and promotion is
one of them.' She swallowed and drew in a long, calming
breath, forcing herself to take it easy, to not fall to pieces
in front of him.

'My career isn't as important to me as Ruthie is,' she of-
fered more calmly. 'I'm sorry, John. I didn't mean to snap.
You helped me out years ago. You were there for me when
I needed someone and I will be forever grateful to you.'

'But you wish I'd butt out of your personal life, especially now we're going to be working together?'

Mackenzie sighed and nodded. 'We really don't know
that much about each other. I mean, I've only just found
out that your parents have died and that you have sisters.'

'Plus a gaggle of nieces and nephews. Why do you think
I like working on the other side of the world?' He smiled at
her and Mackenzie instantly felt her knees begin to buckle.
Why did he have to be so darned handsome? So darned
nice? So darned considerate?

She'd been able to tell from the tone of his voice and
the smile behind his eyes that he absolutely adored his sib-
lings and she couldn't help the pang of envy that passed
through her. 'They sound horrible. No doubt they meddle
in your life simply because they care.'

'Aha. You've met them.' John's smile had increased to
full wattage and she took a step back, putting out a hand
to the wall in order to support herself against his powerful presence. 'Listen, Mackenzie.' His tone was soft and
the smile slowly disappeared from his lips.

'I didn't come here to confuse you. I came to Sunshine

General for the job. I shouldn't have surprised you the way I did in Theatre. I really was only trying to help out and I didn't think of how it might emotionally affect you. Seeing someone from your past, especially from a tragic time in your life, is never easy to cope with. You were unprepared and I apologise.'

At his heartfelt speech, Mackenzie simply stared at him, becoming lost in his glorious blue eyes or intently watching the way his perfect mouth formed the words. Belatedly she realised it was her turn to speak but before she could nudge her mind back into gear, think of some sort of appropriate response and then quickly escape to the female changing rooms, which were just around the corner, John took a small step forward and gently brushed a hair away from her cheek.

The small, insignificant touch caused her to gasp, her lips parting with trembling anticipation. When his gaze dipped to momentarily stare at her mouth, Mackenzie's heart began to hammer wildly against her ribs. 'Uhh…' She'd tried to speak, then had stopped and cleared her throat. 'Thanks.'

'For?' He stepped even closer and leaned with one hand on the wall just to her right.

Mackenzie looked up, their gazes still locked in some silent conversation, engaging in a language they both spoke fluently but for whatever reason hadn't spoken for quite a number of years. 'Um…everything?'

The corners of his lips curved upwards. 'Everything, eh? Makes me sound like quite a guy.' The teasing lilt of his words caused her to relax, just a fraction, before she returned his smile.

'You know what I mean,' she ventured, pleased to find the strength in her legs was beginning to return. She eased away from the wall and John dropped his arm and took a step back. It was then both of them seemed to realise they'd been standing in the middle of one of the hospital corridors almost flirting with each other. In fact, Mackenzie realised after she quickly excused herself and headed to the changing rooms, they hadn't been *almost* flirting—they *had* been flirting.

She'd been flirting with John Watson. The man who had rescued her. The man who was her new boss! What did it mean? Even as she'd stood beneath the spray of the shower, washing off the arduous stint in theatre, she tried to wrap her head around the concept that she was indeed highly attracted to John.

In the past, she'd always looked on him as her knight in shining armour. He'd been there to see her through the darkest time of her life. She'd been in his arms several times, she'd held his hand without question or ulterior motive, she'd kissed his cheek with gratitude. Why was it now so incredibly different?

As she stood beside him at the recovery nurses' station, reading the quick, perfectly legible notes he'd entered into Mrs Windslow's file, given the lead surgeon had been unconscious, Mackenzie wished she wasn't so aware of him. She tried instead to focus on what she needed to write, on how Mrs Windslow's operation had progressed right up until the moment she'd looked into John's eyes and passed out.

She moaned with embarrassment and shook her head.

'Something wrong?' he asked.

'I can't believe I passed out like that.'

'It's not the preferred method for conducting a successful surgical procedure,' he teased gently, and she laughed.

'What a day.'

'Almost done? Do you have clinic this afternoon?'

'Yes.'

'And Ruthie?' He lowered his voice and glanced across at her. 'Who looks after Ruthie while you're here? Does the hospital have a childminding centre? If not, that's one thing I'm more than happy to fight for.'

Mackenzie held up her hands to stop him. 'Whoa, there, boy. They do and it's a great centre. Ruthie used to go there when she was younger but now I've found a lovely family day-care lady called Grandma Liz, who is indeed a grandmother figure and a lovely woman who adores Ruthie.' Mackenzie checked her watch. 'And if I don't get a wriggle on, I'll be late for pick-up.' She finished writing up Mrs Windslow's notes.

John wrote down a few notations in the file he was holding before closing it. 'How does Ruthie cope with your working hours?'

Mackenzie shrugged. 'The same as any child being raised by a sole parent. She complains sometimes but it's only since she started school that she's realised she's different from other children who have two parents. Until then, she had no idea she was living what some would term a different sort of life.' She closed Mrs Windslow's file. 'Still, I'm determined to make her life far better than the one I had, which, I think, is all any parent can ever do for their child.'

'Agreed. Parents should do everything they can for their children, especially when they're young,' John remarked softly, then took another set of casenotes from the cabinet and opened them up. He wrote a few lines, signed his name then turned to face Mackenzie.

Part of him wanted to tell her more about his past but he simply wasn't used to discussing it. His sisters had sucked all the talk out of him when tragedy had struck his life so many years ago. They'd discussed and they'd analysed and all the while, even though he'd known they loved him, it had felt like they were content to keep pouring lemon juice into the open wound of his heart, which hadn't promoted any sort of healing. It was why he now travelled so extensively.

He exhaled slowly, looking into Mackenzie's green eyes, his mouth going dry as he honestly contemplated telling her about his past, about the tragedy that had changed his life for ever. 'Mackenzie,' he began, and took her hand in his.

'Yes, John?'

'I…er…' He stopped, swallowing compulsively as he tried to make the words spring forth to his lips. 'All those years ago, when I…helped you and…' He stopped for a moment, closing his eyes. He was surprised when she gave his hand a little encouraging squeeze.

'John, you don't have to tell me anything if you don't want—'

'But I *do* want to.' He exhaled again and shook his head. 'It's just a little more difficult than I'd realised.' John looked down at their hands, joined together, and couldn't resist rubbing his thumb over her knuckles. He'd done the same thing all those years ago when he'd been trying to give her courage, to help her to believe in herself, to empower her, but now it truly felt as though she was giving him the same emotions in return.

'Mackenzie.' He dragged in another deep breath, determined to try again. He was about to place his other hand on top of hers when one of the nursing staff came into the area. Mackenzie instantly removed her hand and started fussing about the place, tidying up notes and putting pens away.

'I appreciate you offering to help me decipher the paperwork on the present research projects in the department,' John remarked as he returned the casenotes to the cabinet. 'I'll meet you in my office in…' he checked his watch, his tone brisk and extremely businesslike '…ten minutes.' Without another word, he turned and headed out of Recovery, leaving Mackenzie to wonder what had just happened. She hadn't promised anything about research projects, although if he needed help in that area she was more than happy to provide it, but he also knew she had to leave the hospital to go and collect Ruthie.

She quickly finished up in Recovery, a little preoccupied with thinking of what he'd been on the verge of telling her. What could he have been about to say? She pressed 'pause' on her wayward thoughts as she headed to ICU, and after being satisfied that her patients were progressing well, she quickly headed to the orthopaedic department. None of the secretaries were in and as she walked towards John's new office, she realised the door was wide open.

He was standing at his desk, shuffling papers around, as though he really was trying to make sense of the workload he'd inherited from the person who'd been acting director for the past six months. She took the opportunity to watch him for a moment, liking the way his strong and clever hands quickly sorted and ordered. Within a matter of seconds even she could see some wood peeking out beneath the white paper.

'Paperless office,' she heard him mutter, and couldn't help but smile. She must have made a sound because he immediately looked up and caught her standing there. 'Will you just look at this?' He spread his arms wide, indicating his desk. Mackenzie took a few steps into his office.

'And you were wondering why I *didn't* want the job?'

'You're a smart woman, Mackenzie. I've always thought that about you.'

'So.' She took another few steps towards his desk. 'Do you really need help with the research projects?'

'I wouldn't mind but it can wait until some time during the next week or two. I don't know why I said that. I guess I just panicked when the nurse came into the nurses' station and I wanted to quickly provide a reason why we might have been standing so close, talking so softly.'

'Holding hands,' she pointed out.

'It was stupid of me.'

Her smile brightened. 'Totally.'

'Anyway,' he said as he put a few manila folders into a briefcase then pulled out a small set of keys, 'right now it's time for me to meet your daughter.'

'My—' Mackenzie gaped at him.

'Ruthie. You're going to introduce me to Ruthie.'

CHAPTER FOUR

'WHY WOULD I do that?' she asked, watching John head towards the door and indicate that she should precede him out. She did, still a little stunned at his words, as she watched him lock his office door then head to the stairwell. There, he held the door for her again, waiting for her to go through.

'Because I'm interested to see her. There's a special place in my heart for little Ruthie. As an orthopod, we rarely get a chance to deliver babies and although I wasn't going to tell you at the time, Ruthie's was the first delivery I'd ever taken the lead on, without a trained obstetrician looking over my shoulder.'

'Excuse me? *You* took the lead?' she queried with the finest thread of haughtiness in her tone as she started descending the stairs. 'I beg to differ, John, because I am fairly certain *I* was the one taking the lead. Besides, by the time Ruthie was actually ready to be delivered, you had a paramedic with you and all the equipment in the ambulance.'

'And I have been thankful for the paramedics' timely arrival ever since,' he quickly interjected.

'I know.' The haughtiness disappeared from her voice and she sighed. 'Me, too, because if we'd still been sitting by that tree, in the middle of the scrub, in the fading light…' She stopped and shuddered. 'Actually, I don't want to think about the "what ifs" because they didn't happen and thanks to your *assistance* during her delivery, Ruthie is now a healthy, happy and, if I do say so myself, well-adjusted little girl.'

'Exactly what every little girl should be.' His deep words echoed around the stairwell. They descended one floor and continued heading down to the next level, John's body much closer to hers than it had been before, his long legs easily taking the stairs much faster than her own, bringing them into a closer, more confined proximity than she'd realised.

She could almost feel the heat radiating from his torso, which wasn't too far from her back. She gripped the hand-rail, knowing she needed to concentrate on her physical movements rather than the way John's nearness was beginning to penetrate her senses.

'What is that scent you're wearing?' The words seemed to rush out of him unbidden, but even so they caused a wave of tingles to spread down Mackenzie's spine. She was headily aware of his own spicy scent, teasing her in return. 'Some sort of flower?'

'Er…it might be,' she said, suddenly unable to think straight, especially when he was so near, clouding her thoughts. 'Or it might be something else. Sandalwood or vanilla. I'm not sure.' She shrugged a shoulder as though to confirm her indecision. 'It was a gift from Bergan for my birthday.'

'Ah, yes.' John nodded. 'Your birthday. That was only a few weeks ago, right?'

Mackenzie glanced back up at him for a moment but wished she hadn't because it only made her realise just how close their bodies were in the empty stairwell. She cleared her throat. 'Memorised my personnel file?'

'No.'

'Then how could you possibly—?'

'Do you have any idea, Mackenzie, just how many times patients are required to provide their date of birth in a hospital environment? It's the way we always check we have the right person. Full name and date of birth.'

Mackenzie thought fast for a moment then nodded as realisation dawned. 'The night Ruthie was born. Once we'd arrived at the children's hospital in Sydney, you would have heard me giving my date of birth several times over.'

'Correct.'

'And you remembered?'

John took a few steps at a time in order to get ahead of her and open the door to hold it for her. As she passed him she held his gaze, their two bodies drawing closer together. 'It's burned into my memory.' His words were soft, his lips barely moving, and the intimacy did nothing to help dispel the tension thickening in the air around them. It was as though they'd been captured in a secluded bubble, completely separate from the world around them.

Why was it when she was near him, near the man who had been there for her during the worst moments of her life, that time seemed to stand still? They were connected by the past but now that John was going to be a part of her present things were definitely beginning to change. For a start, she was positive this repressed level of sensual tension had not existed between them five years ago, yet now it seemed the most natural thing in the world that John should be the man to set her heart alight.

As she stared into his mesmerising blue eyes, their scents intertwining and mingling together to form a heady combination, she was overwhelmed by a sense of inevitability. His gaze dipped momentarily to visually caress her lips before he swallowed.

'Happy belated birthday, Mackenzie,' he murmured, his tone deep, personal, intimate.

There it was again. That flash of awareness, of longing, of desire. Was it real? Did he feel it too or was he just being his usual charming self?

'Thank you,' she said softly. She watched as he swallowed, looking at his smooth neck, his firm jaw and back to his hypnotic eyes. What was this new and incredibly powerful sense she was feeling? With one intense glance he'd managed to send her senses into overdrive, her knees to jelly, her heart pounding fiercely in her chest. What on earth was this new...thing that seemed to exist between them? And how had it happened so quickly?

'Mackenzie.' Her name was a caress on his lips and the realisation that he *did* feel this awkward but powerful tug was enough to scare her. If it had just been her silly schoolgirl fantasies taking her on a merry journey, she would have been able to cope, able to find a way to control it. Besides, she wasn't looking for any type of relationship or involvement with any man right now, and especially not one who already knew her vulnerabilities.

'Ruthie.' Her daughter's name was dragged from her and it was enough to snap her back to reality. She gave her head a little shake as though to clear it. 'Uh...I need to pick up Ruthie.' With that, she continued past him, dragging air into her lungs, only belatedly realising she'd been holding her breath.

'Yes. Ruthie. Good.' He walked briskly beside her. 'So you're OK with me meeting her?'

Mackenzie's sigh was long and deep but eventually she nodded. 'I guess.' She tried to think through the logistics of the rest of her morning and realised she definitely had a very full day planned. 'How about tomorrow?'

'Why not now? I've got time.'

She stopped walking and turned to face him, ensuring there was a bit of distance between them as she gave him a look of annoyance. 'Well, I don't. Look, John, I'm tired and grumpy and I only have a limited amount of time with Ruthie this morning before she has to go to school. I haven't seen her since five o'clock yesterday afternoon and I'm quite possessive of the time I spend with her.'

He nodded, suitably chastised. He'd been wrong to try and pressure her but it had told him one thing—that Mackenzie Fawles was as strong-minded and as determined as she'd been the last time they'd met. 'Quite right. Sorry.' He held up his hands, palms facing her. 'In your own time.'

His understanding and apology knocked the frown from her face. 'I'll…um…think of something and check my schedule and let you know.'

'Good. Thanks. I appreciate it.' The smile returned to his blue eyes and for a moment she stared at him, wondering if he'd looked this incredibly handsome five years ago? She was fairly certain he had but back then her thoughts had most definitely been elsewhere.

'Go, Dr Fawles. Pick up your daughter and enjoy the time you have with her this morning.'

'OK.' She took two steps away from him then looked back, unable to believe how alone and forlorn he appeared. John? Forlorn? It wasn't a word she would have usually equated with a man who had always been such a tower of strength within her mind but as she looked at him she belatedly remembered that he'd only just come to this part of the country and probably didn't know too many people.

'Er…what about you?' she found herself asking. 'Big plans for the day?'

He shrugged and patted his briefcase. 'Paperwork. And a few other little errands.'

'Well…OK.' She jerked her thumb over her shoulder,

indicating the doors just behind her, unable to understand why she was feeling disappointed at not being able to spend more time with him. She shook the feeling off and nodded once. 'So, boss, I guess I'll see you around.'

His smile was bright. 'I guess you will.'

With that she turned and walked towards the doors, telling herself not to look back. She had no reason to be concerned about John Watson. Yes, he'd come back into her life as suddenly as he'd left it and, yes, he was still as handsome as ever and, yes, she couldn't help but feel all tingly inside when she thought of him, but that didn't mean she was his keeper. He was a grown man, used to doing his own thing, and she needed to focus and do her own, too. Colleagues. That's all they were now. Just colleagues.

Mackenzie fished her keys from her bag and unlocked her car but even as she sat behind the wheel of the small, compact car, she knew for a fact that she was lying to herself one hundred percent.

John slid the key into his hotel-room door and opened the door slowly before stepping inside. The room's curtains were still closed, casting a darkness into the room, which belied the fact it was early morning. He didn't bother switching on the light, allowing the quiet stillness to seep into him. The impersonal hotel room completely suited his mood at the moment. Indifferent. Detached. Alone.

He'd never been too bothered with being alone and, in fact, over the past eight years he'd become quite comfortable with his own sense of loneliness, even when he had been surrounded by hundreds of people. The void left by his wife Jacqueline and his daughter Mune-hie had slowly started to ache less, although that one central part of their essence would no doubt stay with him for ever, no matter what might happen in his life.

Ever since he'd first met Mackenzie, having dropped into her life at such a crucial time, he'd started to realise that perhaps he'd withdrawn a bit too much from society in general. Of course he was happy to work in different medical situations, helping people out and doing his job, but with Mackenzie he had become instantly embroiled in her world, assisting with the delivery of her daughter as well as delivering the news of her husband's death.

That one incident had made him realise that if he didn't start connecting with the world again, he was bound to lose himself completely. Even though Mackenzie may feel he'd been the one to support her, in reality her circumstances and her easy acceptance of him had led towards his epiphany—that it was time to start re-engaging with the world.

Over the years he'd even managed the occasional date with a female colleague but he'd always steered clear of any long-term entanglements and he'd been one hundred percent positive he'd had his life firmly under control... until his world had once more collided with Mackenzie's.

When he'd started his new job a few days ago he'd been given a list of the employees attached to Sunshine General's orthopaedic department and her name had most certainly jumped out at him. He'd quickly riffled through the large stack of personnel files he'd been provided to confirm that it was indeed the same woman. He'd opened it and looked at the small hospital identification photograph glued to a piece of paper along with her personal information.

When he'd first seen her picture he'd been happy, intrigued and quite delighted to be able to make her acquaintance once more. He'd also been pleasantly surprised to read her marital status as 'single'.

After that, he'd checked the roster and had been a tad disappointed to discover she was on days off. Going into her theatre had been a conscious decision, not only to see if she required any help after the hectic spate of operations caused by the multiple vehicle pile-up on the motorway but also to catch a glimpse of her. He'd noticed she was firm and in control of the theatre and a smile had appeared on his lips beneath his mask. Same old Mackenzie.

She was a woman from his past. Nothing more, and yet he'd been puzzled why he'd needed to see her so badly. Five years ago he'd felt privileged to help her but since meeting her again it was clear, even after a few short hours, that things had definitely changed…or had that frighteningly natural chemistry existed between them all those years ago, buried so deeply that neither of them had noticed it?

She'd been grieving. He'd been giving her a reassuring shoulder to lean on. He could clearly recall what it had felt like to hold her in his arms, to hold her hand, to brush a lock of hair from her forehead, but all of that had been done with indifferent concern. At least, that's what he'd told himself at the time and while, back then, he'd honestly had no ulterior motive other than to assist her in any way he could, his concern and interest for her well-being had been…intense.

'She was different from other women, even back then.' He spoke the soft words into the quiet room, shaking his head. Why hadn't he realised it? The undercurrents had all been there, the little spark that had shot up his arm when she'd taken his hand in hers. He'd ignored it. Of course he had. She'd been going through the lowest point in her life and he prided himself on being the epitome of an English gentleman.

'She's not at a low point now,' he muttered, making his way through the room towards the balcony. He opened the curtains and unlocked the door, stepping out into the bright Maroochydore sunshine. That's exactly what it had felt like when he'd sat opposite Mackenzie in that crowded hospital cafeteria—as though she'd pulled back the curtains of his hidden heart and unlocked the door with her beautiful smile.

John leaned his elbows on the rail and brought his hands to his face, ignoring the sounds of early-morning life on the busy streets below. He'd wanted to kiss Mackenzie. Even acknowledging this information brought the slow fire burning inside him roaring to life. It was as though an attraction seemed to have sprung up from the depths of the past, something he'd buried deep, but seeing the reciprocal light in her gaze as her eyes had widened at whatever it was that buzzed between them, it had now brought curiosity to see where this attraction might lead.

The pull he felt towards her was already too strong for him to ignore and he could tell she was as puzzled by it as he was. He could easily recall that small frown that would pucker her brow, as he'd seen her wear that expression quite a lot five years ago when she'd looked at him and spread her arms wide, feeling hopelessly out of her depth and completely lost.

'What do I do now?' she'd asked him, sniffing and blowing her nose with a tissue, as they'd waited for news on Ruthie's surgery. 'My husband is…' She'd stopped, her lower lip quivering. 'And Ruthie…' She'd shaken her head and raised a trembling hand to her mouth, her brow crinkling.

John had crossed the room and taken both her hands firmly in his before looking into her sad, beautiful eyes. They may have been red from crying, reflecting fear, confusion and uncertainty, but the colour had still been as vibrant as ever. The most turbulent green, sometimes looking as stormy as the sea and at other times glistening like the purest and most stunning emerald. He'd seen her inner strength, witnessed it during Ruthie's turbulent birth. He'd been able to sense it was there and all she'd really required from him had been the confidence and courage to move forward.

'You...' he'd said, giving her hands an encouraging little squeeze. 'You will cry. You will relive moments over again and again. You'll play the "if only" game and then you'll start to accept.'

'Is that what you do?' she'd asked him, gazing into his eyes, her entire facial expression radiating desperation. She'd needed someone to tell her she would be all right and although it may have sounded like a platitude, John had firmly believed every word he'd said to her.

'Yes,' he'd replied softly. 'Time is a great healer but sometimes it passes awfully slowly.'

She'd nodded at his words and drawn in a deep, cleansing breath. 'One step at a time?'

'Yes.'

'The first step,' she'd said, letting go of his hands and looking at the clock on the wall, 'is to find out what's happening with my daughter.'

'She'll be fine. Ruthie's a fighter. Like her mother.' He'd smiled at her. 'Of that much, I'm absolutely certain.'

And it appeared he'd been right, if what Mackenzie had told him was anything to go on. He was glad she was going to allow him to meet her daughter, to allow her new boss to infiltrate her life once more, because she could quite easily have kept him well away from little Ruthie.

His cellphone rang and he quickly went to answer it, almost hoping it might be Mackenzie, calling to talk to him. Although why would she? He was just someone from her past who was now in her present.

'Dr Watson.'

'Hello, Dr Watson. I'm Prudence, Dr Leyton Abercrombie's personal assistant. I have some more forms the CEO requires you to peruse and sign. I'll email them through to you now so you can start reading and courier a hard copy over to your hotel for the signature.'

John tried not to be disappointed it wasn't Mackenzie and instead forced himself to concentrate on work. Once the call was done, he collapsed onto the bed and rested his hands behind his head, staring at the beige ceiling. Why was he behaving like an adolescent schoolboy where Mackenzie was concerned? Perhaps it was that look she'd given him when they'd exited the stairwell, the look that had let him know that whatever it was that presently existed between them, she felt it, too.

Mackenzie lay on her bed, one hand behind her head, the other twirling her cellphone round and round on the duvet. Should she call him? If she did, what would she say? What possible reason could she give for calling?

'Oh, hi, John. I just wanted to hear that deep and sensual voice of yours once more, the voice I've imagined in my head over the years, especially when I was down or upset or just needed someone to be there for me. Yes, *your* voice. The one that told me all those years ago that I was a person of worth, that I was strong, that I would survive. Those deep, smooth, British tones washing over me, telling me not to lose hope.

'How I've dreamed of your voice, John. How I've dreamed of *you*, John. Do you know that I consider you my own knight in shining armour? No? I didn't think so. You see, John, you were there when I needed you most. You rescued me and you helped me in ways I don't think you'll ever fully comprehend, and the words "thank you" don't feel at all adequate to cover the difference you've made in my life.'

Mackenzie whimpered and closed her eyes. As if she

could call him and say all that! She may have been completely thrown by his appearance in her theatre, stunned enough to faint, but she didn't need to heap more embarrassment on her own shoulders by calling him up and confessing such things.

After she'd spent time with Ruthie and then walked her to school, she'd returned home and had actually called the hospital switchboard and requested John's cellphone number. She'd felt highly self-conscious doing such a thing, even though it wasn't an uncommon occurrence for her to ask for such information of a fellow colleague. John was her new boss and, as such, it was only right she should be requesting his contact details.

When her phone shrilled to life, she almost levitated off the bed, immediately thinking it was John calling *her*, before she realised the ring tone was the one she'd programmed for Bergan.

'Hey.'

'You're not sleeping yet? Or did I wake you?'

'Is there a problem?'

'No. No. Just overtired staff from dealing with so many emergencies but we're all back to normal down here in A & E now.'

'Good to hear it.'

'And speaking of hearing things, I've recently been told that you fainted this morning. Is everything OK, Kenz?'

Mackenzie closed her eyes, unable to believe she was the topic of gossip, but what else could she expect? It wasn't every day one of the surgeons passed out in Theatre. 'I'm fine.'

'Too many hours on your feet and not enough food in your belly?'

She smiled at the mothering tone in Bergan's voice. The two of them had been friends for a very long time and if there was one person she told the truth to, it was Bergan. 'I hope that's the story that's circulating around the hospital.'

'Why? What's the real story?' She could hear the interested tone in Bergan's words.

'John Watson.'

'Ahh…so it *is* the same man. I was told at a heads of department meeting last week that the new orthopaedic director was a man named John Watson.'

'What? You could have given me a heads-up, instead of our eyes meeting across a crowded operating theatre and me passing out.'

Bergan tried not to laugh but failed. 'Sorry, Kenz, but it's not an uncommon name and I have been sort of snowed under with work and—'

'All right, all right. I forgive you.'

'That was easy.' Bergan chuckled. 'So? How does John Watson look five years on?'

'As devastatingly handsome as ever.'

'Yeah, he was a bit of a looker, wasn't he? Not *my* type at all. At any rate, your knight in shining armour is back in your life, startling you in Theatre and signing on as the new head of department. The big question is, what does all this mean for you? It's not like you to faint, Kenz.'

'I don't know what it means,' she wailed, confusion and despair evident in her tone. 'I…we…um…shared…moments.'

'Moments of what? I don't understand.'

'*Moments* moments,' she tried to clarify. 'Like I can't stop thinking about him moments.'

'Really?' Mackenzie could hear the slow delight in her friend's voice. 'That *is* interesting. And did John give you any indication that he was sharing these same…*moments*?'

For some strange reason she couldn't stop the excited trembling in her tone as she said, 'Yes.'

'*Very* interesting. So…what are you going to do about it?'

Mackenzie closed her eyes and shook her head from side to side on the pillow in total confusion. 'I have absolutely *no* clue!'

CHAPTER FIVE

TWO DAYS AFTER John Watson had burst back into her life, Mackenzie made the firm decision to seek him out once they'd finished the orthopaedic clinic for the day but the moment clinic was over, she had an attack of the nerves. To stave them off, she went to the ward and checked on her patients, pleased to see Mrs Windslow was progressing nicely. Next, she took a detour to the maternity ward to admire Sonny's new baby boy, congratulating him and his wife on the fine addition to their family.

Finally, she knew she couldn't put it off any longer and made her way to John's office. She'd decided that it was better to get the meeting between him and her daughter out of the way sooner rather than later. Over the past few days they'd seen each other at ward rounds and inter-departmental meetings and, thankfully, John hadn't pressured her at all about the prospect of exactly when she was going to allow him to make the acquaintance of her daughter.

As she walked through the orthopaedic department towards his office, she couldn't help but feel as though the administration staff were looking at her, watching her, knowing exactly what her motive was for seeking out the new orthopaedic director. In reality, everyone else in the department was packing up, getting ready to head home for the day.

Mackenzie shook the thoughts from her head, realising she was being foolish once more, and quickly checked with John's secretary that it was all right for her to go into John's office.

'Should be fine,' the woman told her, as she picked up her handbag and made for the door. Mackenzie knocked once, before opening the door and stepping in to find John sitting behind his desk, talking on the phone. She mumbled an apology and was about to exit again when he called her name and beckoned her closer.

'OK. Great. Thanks for that information.' A pause. 'Yes. It's good to get all the red tape done and out of the way. I appreciate both your help and that of your staff, Leyton. OK. Have a good night.' With that, John replaced the receiver.

'The hospital's CEO making sure you're all settled in?' she asked, coming a little closer towards his desk.

'Something like that. Now, to what do I owe the pleasure of this visit to my office?'

'Well…John, you said you wanted to meet…my daughter and…' Mackenzie couldn't believe how tongue-tied she felt and stopped to clear her throat.

'Now?' He quickly stood and closed a few of the files on his desk. 'I'm ready if you are.'

'Just like that?' She was astounded at his eagerness.

'I'm not about to look a gift horse in the mouth, although wherever it is we're going we'll need to take your car because I still haven't found the time to lease one yet.'

'You've been here almost a week,' she pointed out as he packed his briefcase and turned off his desk lamp.

'And it's been a rather busy one.'

'OK, but I think I should warn you. My car is rather small.'

'I'm sure I'll cope.' He held out his hand towards the door. 'Shall we?'

'Well, if you're sure...'

'I'm sure. I've wanted to meet Ruthie for a long time, Mackenzie.' His tone was firm yet there was softness to his words.

'Of course.' She headed out of his office and glanced at the nearby stairwell door. The thought of being in such close proximity to him once more as they exited the hospital filled her with nervousness she was having a difficult time keeping under control.

'Actually, I just have a few things to do so why don't I meet you out the front of the hospital in...two or three minutes?' She started off down the corridor at a brisk pace, desperately needing some breathing room from his deliciously overpowering presence, giving him no opportunity to reply.

The fact that he'd been so eager, so willing and ready to go and meet Ruthie the second she'd suggested it, indicated that he had indeed been thinking about it over the past few days but had been polite and gentlemanly enough not to pressure her on the subject. It only made her appreciate him even more.

Mackenzie sighed as she took a different route to the front of the hospital, desperately trying to get her emotions under control. In many ways she knew John intimately. She knew what it was like to be held in his arms, to feel his hand reassuringly in hers, to lean her head on his shoulder, to hear his unwavering voice telling her everything was going to be OK. There had been truth in all his expressions and she'd trusted him implicitly, but in other ways she felt she knew next to nothing about him.

'Perhaps you can rectify that,' she told herself as she spied him standing at the front of the hospital, briefcase

in hand, as he waited for her. The sight of him caused her
heart to do a little flip of delight and she worked hard to
ensure her breathing was as normal as possible because
right now, with him standing there in his navy trousers,
white shirt and colourful tie, his hair being ruffled by the
wind, she felt like hyperventilating.

'Hi. Sorry about that. Just a few little things that
needed…you know…fixing.' She had no idea what she
was saying so when all he did was smile at her, those hypnotic eyes of his making her knees begin to weaken, she
immediately turned and started walking towards the car
park, knowing he'd follow.

The sun was starting to set, the sky a lovely mix of
reds, pinks and blues. 'It's beautiful here,' John remarked.

'It is.' Feeling that wasn't enough of an answer and
wanting to keep the conversation going so she didn't feel
so conscious of every move he made, she added, 'Er…what
made you decide to come here?'

'The job. I don't really know anyone here on the Sunshine Coast. Except you.'

'Oh?' They reached her car and she unlocked it, trying
not to smile as John folded his tall frame into her small car.

'And soon I'll know Ruthie.' He smiled brightly. 'I can't
thank you enough for agreeing to this, Mackenzie. I'm
looking forward to it.'

'Uh…OK, then.' And he really was, she realised. It
wasn't just a line. Over the past five years her friends Bergan, Regina and Sunainah had encouraged her to date and
she'd become an expert at spotting when men were trying
to feed her a line. Reggie had been the main culprit in the
set-ups, organising several blind dates.

A few had gone well but the instant they'd found out
she was a sole parent, that she had a young daughter, most
of them would high-tail it out of the restaurant faster than

you could say, 'Cheque, please!' Yet as she drove along, she could see that John really was delighted at the prospect of getting to know Ruthie.

How she managed to drive, she had no idea. Concentrating on the road was nigh on impossible with John sitting beside her in the passenger seat, his knees bent uncomfortably in her small car.

As though he could sense her unease, he kept up a steady stream of chatter about nothing in particular but somehow had her laughing all the same. How did he do that? Put someone at ease so quickly? Get them to trust him? Make them feel as though they were the most important person in the world?

She thought back to when they'd first met and she'd been in such dire straits and John had saved the day. He'd held her hand while she'd had contractions, he'd kept her calm when she'd been gripped by a rising sense of panic, he'd held her securely in his arms while she'd wept on hearing the news that Warick hadn't survived the accident.

'It's OK. I'm here. We'll get through this together.'

He couldn't possibly have any idea just how much she'd wanted him to say those words to her over and over again throughout the past five years. There had been so many times when she'd felt completely unable to cope juggling a young toddler and a demanding career. All too often, she'd curled up in her bed, with Ruthie sleeping beside her, and wish for John's strong arms to hold her. For his deep, reassuring voice to rumble through her entire body, making her feel secure and important. She'd needed his strength, his optimism and his reassurance.

As he sat beside her now, scrunched into the seat, she couldn't deny the tug of sensual emotion she felt for him, or the way just being in his presence could make her smile so brightly. She glanced at him again, grinning.

'What?' he asked as she changed lanes and exited the freeway.

'What do you mean, "what"?'

'Why are you smiling at me like that?'

Mackenzie laughed. 'Because you look very funny. Like one of those circus clowns who cram themselves into tiny cars.'

John looked from her to his knees and then hunched over further in the seat, bringing his knees even higher. 'How's this?' He smiled at her and Mackenzie couldn't help but laugh again at the sight he made. 'All I'm missing is the little bowler hat with a flower coming out of it.'

'That can be arranged.' She shook her head, marvelling at how incredibly different he was from Warick. Her husband had been the ultimate corporate businessman. Three-piece suits, working lunches and dinners. Networking, networking, networking. When he'd seen something he'd wanted, he'd focused all his energies on gaining it. That's how he'd finally won her over, persistent with his romancing, making her believe this was the real him until after the wedding, when she'd discovered he'd wanted a professional wife so they could be a professional couple. Introducing her to his colleagues as Dr Fawles had given him a big thrill.

'Plus, you're a knockout. Brains and beauty. I'm the envy of every guy in the office and the boss is finally starting to take my ideas for overseas expansion seriously.'

It had always been work, work, work with Warick and he'd been rather annoyed when she'd told him about the pregnancy. Still, his boss had approved of him becoming a 'family man' so Warick had played the doting father-to-be whenever they'd been in public. Privately, though, he'd been married to his job rather than her.

Arrogant, selfish and highly insecure, he'd never gone

out of his way to be silly, to make her laugh, to make a
fool of himself in order to bring a smile to her face. John,
however, seemed to be such an intense giver, *wanting* to
make others happy, *wanting* to support them, *wanting* them
to gain the most out of their lives.

Whatever his motives were, she'd most certainly ben-
efited. He'd left a lasting mark on her life, a positive one,
and even though she'd yearned for his thoughtful, supportive presence, it had been in remembering his words that
had helped her to start again.

'You're a strong woman, Mackenzie Fawles,' she remembered him telling her when she'd stood beside Ruthie's humidi-crib, wondering whether her premature baby
girl was strong enough to make it through the night. 'Don't
ever forget that and don't let anyone else tell you different.'

She sighed, slowing the car as she turned into a driveway that announced the large, rambling house before them
to be 'Grandma Liz's Day-Care'.

'That's a heavy sigh,' he remarked, trying to shift a
little in the seat. She'd thought he'd be out of the car the
instant she stopped in order to stretch his cramped limbs.
Instead, he released his seat belt before shifting in the seat
to face her. 'Are you concerned about me meeting Ruthie?'

'Well…' Mackenzie sighed again, the late wintry sun
making her blonde hair shine beautifully. She'd pulled it
back into a low ponytail but the front layers weren't quite
long enough and a lock had fallen forward down the side
of her cheek. His fingers itched to reach out, to tuck the
silken locks behind her ear. John's gut tightened as he continued to look at her, positive the woman had no idea how
incredibly beautiful she was.

All those years ago she'd needed a friend and he'd felt
privileged to be there for her during her time of need. Of
course he'd realised her beauty but not in the way he did

now. On his first day, when they'd been chatting in the cafeteria over that putrid cup of warm water the hospital was passing off as tea, he had been astonished to discover an increasing awareness towards Mackenzie.

He'd ignored it, trying to pass it off as the effects of a tired and exhausted mind, but later, when she'd stood in the corridor, leaning against the wall, looking up at him with those emerald-green eyes of hers, he'd been flooded with overwhelming desire for a woman he'd previously re-garded as nothing more than a damsel in distress.

Had she felt it, too? He was positive she had because the other day in the stairwell they'd definitely shared another moment and he'd had a difficult time not lowering his head to find out exactly how her perfect lips tasted. Was it their previous intense but platonic connection that was height-ening the sensations passing between them? Even now, as he sat here in the car, looking across at her, admiring the way the sunlight played upon her hair and gave her a sort of ethereal glow, he felt his gut tighten.

'Mackenzie.' He rubbed his hands together, trying des-perately not to give in to the urge to touch her. She was looking at him with a sense of longing as well as confu-sion and bewilderment and it was that which was helping him to remain in control. 'I really appreciate you letting me do this. Er…meeting Ruthie, I mean.'

'I can see it means a lot to you but I'm still not a hun-dred per cent sure *why* you're so eager. I mean, I know you helped deliver her and of course that gives you more than a passing interest in her life but…'

'But?' he prompted when she stopped.

'I can't shake the feeling that you wanting to meet Ruthie has…something to do with what you almost told me the other day. Remember? When we were in Recovery and the nurse came in and interrupted us?' She stopped, sighing and shaking her head, wishing her thoughts wouldn't jumble together like that but instead be more coherent and calm. Then again, she *was* around John and he always managed to muddle her mind simply by being so close to her.

'You're right. It does have something to do with what I was going to say the other day.' He nodded and gave her a lopsided smile. 'Apart from the fact that I honestly feel a unique sort of connection with Ruthie and that I've thought about her quite often over the years, wondering how the two of you were getting on, there is more to it than that.'

Mackenzie sat there, waiting, not wanting to rush him. When she looked into his face, she could almost see him reflecting back into his past. Something terrible must have happened to him, she was sure of it because she'd never forgotten that moment all those years ago when he'd looked into her eyes and said, 'I know what you're feeling.' Had he? Had he known the heart-wrenching pain? The feeling of having no control whatsoever over your own life? The desolation and anguish?

'Mackenzie…' He breathed out slowly but held her gaze. 'I used to be married.'

She nodded, wanting to encourage him. He'd managed to prise open the door to a particular part of his past and she was almost desperate for him to open it a little wider.

'We had a little girl. Well, we adopted a little girl.'

Mackenzie bit her lip, trying to stop her mind from racing ahead to what she already knew was a horrible outcome to what John was telling her.

'My wife couldn't have children. Ovarian cancer,' he offered by way of explanation.

'Oh, John.' The words, filled with instant sadness, were wrenched from her before she could stop them.

'We were working in Tarparnii and there was an accident and little Mune-hie was left an orphan. She was only one year old and her extended family couldn't provide for her. So…we adopted her.'

Mackenzie pursed her lips together and nodded, wanting him to continue but at the same time not wanting to hear the inevitable words of pain. 'Children have a way of bringing so much love.'

'Yes,' he agreed. 'Just as Ruthie has brought you so much love.'

'I've been so blessed.'

'Yes.' He closed his eyes. 'You've been through hardship, a fair enough amount, but now…' He opened his eyes and reached for her hand. 'Jacqueline, my wife, and Mune-hie…' He stopped, his voice choking.

'They passed away,' she stated, finishing the sentence for him, desperate to spare him the pain of speaking those horrible words out loud. It was clear from the reverence in his tone just how much he'd loved them. It also helped her to better understand just why he was so keen to get to know Ruthie.

He cleared his throat and looked down at Mackenzie's hand in his own. 'I don't talk much about my family, Mackenzie. In fact, hardly at all. To anyone.' He raised his gaze to meet hers. 'But with you…I don't know. It's…'

'Different,' she offered.

'Yes.' His tone was softer than before. 'Thank you for allowing me into Ruthie's life. I know it can't be easy for you, always wanting to protect her as best you can.'

'John…how old…?' Mackenzie stopped and breathed out slowly, wanting to ask the questions uppermost in her mind but also not wanting him to think she was prying.

'Would my daughter have been?' he finished for her. 'Yes.'

'Mune-hie would have been almost fourteen. She was just five when she passed away.'

'Oh, John.' Mackenzie gave his hand a squeeze, desperate to give him her deepest sympathies. 'I couldn't even begin to contemplate the loss of...' She stopped and swallowed over the enormous lump in her throat. 'To lose both of them? Your wife and your daughter.' She shook her head in disbelief, really feeling for him, really sharing his pain.

'A fatal epidemic in Tarparnii.'

'Oh, no.' The anguish intensified as she realised he would have watched them slowly slip from his life, while he'd no doubt done everything he possibly could to save them.

John clenched his jaw and looked into her eyes. 'It doesn't seem to get any easier to talk about it, even though it's been eight years.'

'So this is why you move around so much? Going where you're needed, helping others but all the time wanting to put as much distance between yourself and the rest of the world?'

He shrugged one shoulder. 'I guess so. Sometimes...I think about stopping, settling down somewhere, but nowhere seems...I don't know...to be the right place to settle.'

'What about back in England? With your bossy sisters nearby.'

John instantly shook his head. 'While I love them, they're very intense.'

'You see, because I never really had a family, because I was shunted from one foster-place to the next, I find that really difficult to understand. I love being close to Bergan and Reggie and Sunainah. Of having a permanent residence, of providing a home for Ruthie, but...if anything were to happen...'

John eased his hand from hers and shook his head.

'Don't even think such things. The devastation of losing Mune-hie sits on my heart every single day. There isn't one day that goes by where I don't think about her, where I don't want to feel her arms around my neck, holding me tight and laughing as I tickle her, but it's the sound of her laughter, of the happiness she gave us even though it was for such an short period of time, it's the good times I work hard to remember. It's because of those good times that I'm able to function, I'm able to help others.'

Mackenzie had teared up at his words and she sniffed. 'You give so much to others, John. You've already given so much to me. I'm sure you have no idea how much you helped me all those years ago and I am, and always will be, forever grateful.'

'I don't want your gratitude, Mackenzie.' His voice had thickened slightly. 'I want you to live a happy life, which is what you're doing.'

'I still have difficulty learning who to trust but, thanks to you, I'm getting there.'

'Thanks to me?'

She smiled. 'You believed in me, John. All those years ago, standing by Ruthie's humidi-crib, praying she was strong enough to survive the surgery, that she'd grow into the gorgeous girl she has, you told me I'd be OK. You told me I was strong, that you knew I'd be all right.' She nodded. 'You gave me confidence, John, and it's confidence I've drawn on so many times over the years.'

'Really? I had no idea. I was only trying to support you.'

'And you did. You held me up with your big strong arms when I needed it most and whether you want it or not, you have my complete gratitude and respect.'

John glanced at this special woman. 'You've been waiting a long time to say that, haven't you,' he stated.

'I have and I'm really thankful that I've not only been given the opportunity but that you listened.'

'Good.' He exhaled slowly, gazing into her highly expressive eyes, eyes a man could easily lose himself in, and John knew that was exactly what was happening. They'd both been through so much. His gaze dipped to take in her plump lips, lightly parted, as though inviting him to come hither.

Was it possible…? Dare he hope…? It was clear there was an increasing attraction between them, something new, something different, something he was definitely interested in exploring. Was Mackenzie?

He returned to look into her eyes, the small confines of the car making it incredibly easy to bring them into closer proximity.

'John?' His name was a caress upon her perfect lips and as his gaze dipped once more to take in the rose-pink outline of her mouth, the way she was biting her lower lip in confusion and anticipation, he worked harder at attempting to control the overwhelming desire to finally press his mouth to hers.

'John?' She whispered his name again and this time he heard confused uncertainty in her voice. He shook his head, realising he was probably moving way too fast, but for once in his life he was having difficulty keep a tight rein on his emotions where Mackenzie was concerned.

'You're tying me in knots,' he murmured, his words barely audible.

'Oh?' Her eyes widened in surprise and as she breathed out she licked her dry lips, making him clench his hands into fists in an effort to maintain some sort of control. Was John about to kiss her? The same man who had been her rock throughout her greatest time of need? Was this the right thing to do? Should they be doing it at all? The questions swirled around in her mind but found no answers.

His breath mingled with hers and time seemed to stand still. He looked down into her upturned face, unable to believe how incredibly beautiful she was. As though unable to resist any longer, he reached out a hand and brushed the loose lock of hair behind her ear, delighting in the sensation of being able to touch her, even in such a small way.

Five years ago there had been none of these crazy, chaotic and confusing emotions. It had been the last thing John had expected when he'd reread her hospital file the other night. He'd been intrigued to see what she'd accomplished during the past five years, interested to see her again, but never had it crossed his mind that within such a short space of time he'd be intimately drawn to her.

Even with Jacqueline things hadn't moved this fast. They'd been colleagues, then friends and then slowly that friendship had developed into something more. There had been none of this instant attraction that had hit him at various times since his life had once more been connected with Mackenzie's.

Through hooded lashes he looked down at her glorious face. Her soft skin, her rosy cheeks and cute little nose, not to mention her provocative mouth, which was still open slightly, as though desperately waiting for him. With his heart thumping so wildly beneath his ribs, he wasn't sure how much longer he could resist.

'Mummy!'

John pulled back with a start. 'Did you hear that?' He was looking around, staring out the car's front windscreen.

'Mummy! Mummy! You're here!'

'Oh, my goodness.' Mackenzie made to get out of the car quickly but had forgotten about her seat belt, the stern material holding her firmly in place.

'Here,' John said, instantly coming to her rescue by un-clipping the belt. 'There you go.'

'Thanks,' she mumbled, her hand already opening the door, her legs swinging around so she could get out of the small car.

'Ruthie!' she called, and John watched as the brightest and most beaming smile he'd ever seen crossed Macken-zie's face as she knelt down by the front of the car, her arms held wide open as a young girl with shoulder-length blonde ringlets and big green eyes just like her mother's hurtled forward like some sort of ballistic missile.

Mackenzie scooped the girl into her arms and twirled her around, breathing in her daughter's sweet innocence and allowing it to renew her own strength. 'Hello, my scrum-diddly-umptious girl.'

Ruthie giggled at her mother's words, smothering Mac-kenzie's cheek with kisses. 'You're so funny, Mummy.'

'I missed you.' Mackenzie shifted Ruthie to her hip, cradling her close as Ruthie started chattering away, tell-ing her mother everything that had happened since they'd last seen each other, but she immediately stopped short when she realised that a *man* was clambering out of her mother's car.

'Who's *that*?' She pointed and Mackenzie quickly low-ered her daughter's hand.

'It's rude to point, sweet-pea,' she said softly as she watched John's rather clumsy exit from her car. She couldn't help but giggle at the awkward sight made by such a tall man getting out of a small car.

'What's funny?' Ruthie wanted to know, looking from her mother to the man now walking towards them, but Mackenzie didn't reply.

'This is my Ruthie,' Mackenzie told John.

'Hello, there. I'm very pleased to meet you, Ruthie.'

'You talk funny.' Ruthie giggled at his accent.

'Ruthie, this is my…uh…colleague from work….John.' John tried not to smile as Mackenzie stumbled over her words. It was difficult not to when the woman was so naturally charming. 'He comes from England. That's why he speaks differently to us.'

'Cool. Are you a doctor, too?'

'I am.'

'Do you work with my mum? Doing the operations and stuff?'

'Yes, I do. We look after a lot of pa—'

'Wait, wait, wait!' Ruthie demanded, interrupting him, and Mackenzie instantly stopped walking towards the house.

'What, what, what?' she said earnestly.

'I know a story you told me about a man called John.' Her words were firm and direct as she looked from John and then back to her mother. 'He was the man who helped Mummy to make me born.'

'That's right.' Mackenzie nodded. 'This is the same John.'

'You told her about that?' He seemed surprised.

'Of course. Every child has a right to know about their birth, and while Ruthie's was probably a little bit more… dramatic than others, it's still *her* story.'

'You're *my* John?' Ruthie was astounded, looking at him with her little mouth hanging open in astonishment.

'Uh…well…yes. I suppose I am.'

'Mummy told me that if it wasn't for you, if you hadn't come along and helped her, I might have been really sick. You *saved* me.'

John raised his eyebrows at this information and looked at Mackenzie, who shrugged one shoulder. Given her foster-home upbringing, he could well imagine her need to

...as honest with her daughter as possible. ...tell you that she had the hardest part of all?'

...Ruthie's eyes were as big and as wide and as green ...mother's.

'Giving birth is really hard.' John looked from Ruthie back to Mackenzie. 'And your mum was amazing. I was so proud of her.'

At his words, Ruthie tightened her arms around her mother's neck. 'She's the bestest mummy.'

John kept his gaze on Mackenzie, whose sparkling green eyes were wide with astonishment at his praise. 'I can well believe it.' His voice was warm.

Mackenzie wondered how it was possible that he could make her feel all gooey inside simply with a few well-intentioned words? It appeared he still had as much faith in her as he had five years ago but now, added to that mix, there was a hefty dose of mutual attraction too.

As they headed inside to collect Ruthie's things and to say goodbye to Grandma Liz, as Ruthie called her, Mackenzie couldn't help but wonder whether John was happy about their interrupted kiss. Of course the atmosphere inside the small car had been nice and cosy and things had just sort of…happened, but as she glanced at him from time to time it was difficult to get a read on what he might be thinking.

He'd confessed to not being able to settle in one place for too long, always wanting to move around, to try new places and have new experiences, but was the main reason behind that decision to stop himself from putting down roots once more? From opening his heart? From moving on with his life?

She knew how difficult it was to start a new life after the loss of a spouse and while she and Warick may not have had the most perfect of marriages, it had certainly been another big change for her to deal with, but she'd had Ruthie to focus on. John had had no one.

As she drove home, Ruthie chattered away happily in the back seat of the car, telling them both about some of the games she and the other kids had played after school at Grandma Liz's.

'That certainly sounds like a lot of fun,' John responded. 'What else did you do today?'

Ruthie thought for a moment before drawing in a deep breath and saying, '*Well…*' Then she launched into another long spiel about something that had happened at school when one of the boys in her class had laughed so hard at something that he'd made milk come out of his nose.

Although Mackenzie was tired, she was grateful for Ruthie's constant chatter. Usually, after a long day at the hospital, Mackenzie would ask her daughter for a bit of silence as they drove home but today she was ever so grateful to Ruthie for ensuring there wasn't a dull moment. The one thing Mackenzie *was* having difficulty trying to comprehend was the fact that she was presently driving John Watson to her home!

She wasn't the type of person to 'entertain' and rarely invited people back to her town house. The girls—Bergan, Reggie and Sunainah—were definitely the exception but, then, she'd known them for such a long time.

And that was the problem, as far as she could see, where John was concerned. They had a bond, one that had been forged during difficult and tragic circumstances, which meant her relationship with him was completely different not only from that with any of her colleagues but any of the men she'd dated over the past few years.

Her home was her sanctuary, a place where she could throw off her worries and cares and just chill with Ruthie. So why was she pulling into her driveway with John sitting beside her, his knees still scrunched up close to his body, chatting animatedly with her daughter?

She was still reeling from the fact that there was something very different existing between them and the realisation that *both* of them felt it. Even when she'd first started dating Warick, with his practised charm and charisma, she hadn't felt that overwhelming sense of…rightness. She felt it with John, in spades. And *that* was a definite worry, one she wasn't quite sure how to deal with.

She turned into the small cul-de-sac where four identical townhouses stood. She and Ruthie lived at number two, Bergan lived at number four and an elderly couple, the Allingtons, lived at number three. Town-house number one had been on the market for at least the past six months but still had no takers, the large real estate sign starting to look a little faded in the morning sunlight.

Mackenzie quickly switched off the engine and climbed from the driver's seat, the need for space, for some fresh air pressing heavily on her sensibilities. Just focus on your routine, she told herself.

'Don't forget your backpack,' she told her daughter as Ruthie continued to chatter to John, easily taking his big hand in her little one as she led him into their home, desperate to show *her* John her special, sparkly, purple bedroom.

'All my friends like pink but I like purple the best but I sometimes like a little bit of pink because I think they go really nicely together, don't you think so too, John?'

Ruthie continued to chatter and indeed, when she opened the door, John's senses were assailed with a flood of several different shades of purple. Bedsheets, curtains, walls were all purple. The large princess castle rug, which took up most of her floor, was in shades of pinks and purple. Even the fairy-princess netting Ruthie had around her bed was a lovely lilac colour. Only the carpet, which he glimpsed around the edges of the room, thanks to the rug, all the toys, dolls and books scattered here and there, was a beige colour.

'It's such a little girl's room,' he murmured, a slow, sad smile crossing his face.

'Come and look at this, John,' Ruthie demanded, tugging on his hand and drawing him further into the room. She instructed him to sit on her bed and proceeded to introduce him to a few of her dolls.

'And this is Zoe,' she said, unzipping her backpack and pulling out a well-loved doll who was dressed as an angel. 'She's my absolutely favourite. We do everything together.' Ruthie stepped forward and whispered loudly, 'I take her to school in my bag because she really likes going to school but the teacher said I can't have her sitting on my desk because I look at Zoe, not the board, but I can play with her at lunchtime and we have so much fun, don't we, Zoe?'

Ruthie was now addressing her words to the doll in question and much to his shock and surprise John became aware of a rush of emotion flooding through him.

It had been a long time since he'd been surrounded by such things, things that were so perfect for any little girl, just as they'd been perfect for his daughter. He'd thought he'd dealt with his loss, keeping himself busy and occupied and focused on work, on helping others wherever possible, and yet, sitting on the comfortable purple bed, surrounded by similar toys to the ones he and Jacqueline had given Mune-hie when she'd come to live with them, he was swamped with repressed emotions.

It had been their goal to provide for her, to give her a life filled with love and laughter. It had been so difficult not to spoil her, not to buy her the latest toys or clothes simply because it had given them pleasure.

'What's the matter?' Ruthie asked him a moment later. She was standing in the middle of her room, head on the side, watching him closely.

'Er...what do you mean?' John frowned quizzically, not quite sure of the last things Ruthie had said to him as he'd zoned out and taken a trip down memory lane—a lane he'd vowed never to walk down again.

'You're crying.'

'Am I?' John instantly raised a hand to his cheek and was surprised to feel a lone tear sliding down from his eye.

'Why are you crying?'

Mackenzie heard her daughter's words to John just as she reached the top of the stairs. John was crying? What on earth had happened in the past few minutes since she'd left them alone? From where she presently stood on the top stair she could see right into Ruthie's room. John was sitting on the bed and Ruthie was standing on the rug, Zoe held tightly in her hands. Mackenzie was about to walk in when John's next words stopped her.

'Because your beautiful room reminds me of another little girl's room. She liked purple, too.'

'What's her name?' Ruthie asked.

'Her name...was Mune-hie.'

'Moon-hey?' Ruthie repeated.

John smiled at the attempt. 'Close. It's a Tarparniian name. It means "smart and peaceful".'

'That's pretty. Mummy said my names means "friend to everyone" and that's what I am. I'm a friend to everyone. Me and Zoe. We're friends to everyone.' She gave Zoe a little kiss then returned her attention to John. 'So can I see her?'

'Who?'

'Moon-hey.'

'Oh.' John's smile slowly slipped away. 'Er...no. Sorry.'

'But can I be her friend?' Ruthie implored earnestly, and as Mackenzie watched, she felt a lump begin to form in her throat. 'I'm good at making friends.'

'I know, Ruthie, but…um…you see…Mune-hie died. About eight years ago.'

'Oh.' Ruthie nodded as though she completely understood all about death. 'My daddy died but Mummy said he gave her the bestest present ever and that was me.' Ruthie looked down at Zoe, then back to John. 'You can hold Zoe if you want. She'll make you feel better.' She held her most favourite doll, her most prized possession out to him. 'She's a really good friend, too.'

Mackenzie watched as John accepted the doll, holding the raggedy, much-loved thing in his big hands, unsure what to do with it.

'Just hold her close and give her a cuddle,' Ruthie instructed in that bossy way of hers.

John just sat there, looking at the doll.

'No. I said hug her close.' Ruthie was starting to get a little demanding and Mackenzie took that as her cue to make her presence known. She sniffed and cleared her throat before walking towards them, John's gaze instantly melding with hers.

In one brief moment she saw pain, anguish and immense heartbreak. The man had lost his wife and daughter and while he'd no doubt done his best to come to terms with it over the past eight years, sitting and chatting with her five-year-old daughter had clearly brought back a lot of repressed memories.

'How are we doing in here?' Mackenzie asked, her tone a little over-bright. John quickly rose from the bed and handed Zoe back to Ruthie.

'Er…thanks,' he mumbled.

Mackenzie looked at Ruthie, who was hugging the doll

close once more, her wide eyes radiating confusion. 'Princess, can you please go to the toilet and wash your hands then downstairs to the kitchen to set the table for dinner.'

'But I'm showing John all my dolls.'

'*Please*, Ruthie.' There was a sternness in Mackenzie's voice that brooked no argument.

'Okay,' Ruthie returned, and after giving a heavy sigh, Zoe tight in her hands, girl and doll headed off to do their mother's bidding.

'Sorry about that, John. We don't get many new visitors and she's so proud of her room that she shows it off to everyone who walks in the door.' John didn't say anything. Instead, he just stood there, on Ruthie's rug, staring down at the rest of Ruthie's dolls. The silence surrounding them seemed to intensify. 'I…er…overheard what you told Ruthie, about your daughter, I mean.'

'She…er…Mune-hie liked her dolls…' He stopped and swallowed a few times. 'Her room was very frilly and… um…' He stopped again then shook his head.

'I can't do this.'

Mackenzie frowned at his words, concern in her tone. 'Can't do what, John?'

'This!' He indicated the space between them then waved his arms to indicate the entire room.

'I'm not sure—'

He shook his head again. 'I'm sorry, Mackenzie. For everything.'

With that, he stalked from Ruthie's purple room, rushed downstairs and was out the front door so fast she barely had time to go after him.

'John?' she called as she headed outside, but he was already halfway down her street, disappearing from her view.

CHAPTER SIX

JOHN STOOD ON the balcony of his hotel, once more looking down at the busy streets of Maroochydore as the sun began to rise on a new day. He knew that as he was going to be here for quite some time, he'd better get his act together and find somewhere other than the hotel to stay, but things hadn't exactly gone to plan since he'd arrived on the Sunshine Coast.

Mackenzie. He shook his head. When he'd told her she was tying him in knots, he hadn't been joking. John dragged in a breath and pushed his hands through his hair. Between Mackenzie stirring up his hormones and little Ruthie his memories, he wondered if he'd ever get his mind back on track.

He hadn't expected Ruthie's easygoing and accepting nature to open up the box he'd thought he'd nailed shut long ago. Mackenzie's daughter was as sweet and as innocently precious as Mune-hie had been at the same age so it was no wonder he'd almost broken down.

He should probably call Mackenzie and apologise for walking out on her and Ruthie the way he had yesterday evening. He prided himself on being a gentleman and yet he'd displayed such ungentlemanly behaviour. He pulled his cellphone from his pocket, tapping her number into his phone with his thumb. He was about to press 'send' when he remembered she'd be in the process of taking Ruthie to school.

Rolling his eyes, he tossed the phone onto the bed and decided it was probably better for him to go to the hospital and throw himself into work. There was always something to do at the hospital and even though he'd managed to clear some time this morning so he could lease a car and try and find a place to live, if necessary he could put it off a little longer. So long as he could control his thoughts and not think about Mackenzie, he'd be fine.

He went back inside and put some of the work he'd managed to concentrate on last night into his briefcase in preparation for the day. Mackenzie had somehow managed to commandeer his thoughts quite often but now he needed to find his professionalism from somewhere and start to focus on what needed to be done.

He managed to get through his morning shower and order some breakfast before his thoughts returned to her. He'd checked his phone and found he had one missed call. It was Mackenzie's number. Almost like a love-struck teen, he checked his messages, eager to hear her voice once more.

'Hi…er…John. Sorry to bother you. Just wanted to check everything was…you know…OK. If you want to talk, I'm here. Sorry again for…well… Anyway, call me if you want to. Bye.'

'To listen to this message again, please press one,' said the automated voice of the telephone company.

John pressed one and slowly exhaled. 'Mackenzie.' He breathed her name into the silent room, hating himself for causing her consternation. She was kind, generous, thoughtful and clearly devoted to Ruthie. He knew her marriage hadn't been all that happy when her husband had died, Mackenzie having confessed to him as she'd cried on his shoulder that she was sure Warick had been having affairs.

It wasn't like him to speak ill of the dead but what an idiot her husband had been. John knew if he were married to Mackenzie, he would spend all his days trying to make their lives as happy and as fulfilled as possible. He would accept her love as the most precious gift and he'd give her all of his in return. He quickly gave himself a mental shake, clearing such dangerous thoughts.

As the voice message ended for the second time, John disconnected the call and lay back on the bed. He should call her back. Apologise for his behaviour. But what would he say after that? That he'd walked out because her daughter was gorgeous and *alive*? While his daughter had been cruelly taken from him? That being around her and Ruthie reminded him of just how much he'd lost? If he confessed as much, like most women, Mackenzie would probably want to discuss it all in detail, and he simply wasn't in the mood to talk about Mune-hie or Jacqueline.

He picked up his phone and looked at it, knowing that good manners dictated he should return her call, but right now he wasn't too concerned with manners, so when his phone rang again he simply stared at the display.

The caller ID was the same number as his previously missed call. Mackenzie's number. He looked at the digits illuminated on the screen and realised his mouth had gone dry. Maybe he wasn't ready to talk to her, to go into detail, to pour more lemon juice into his old wounds. Clenching his jaw, he ignored the call, knowing it would again go through to voice mail.

Instead, he shoved the phone into his pocket and started packing his briefcase. Work would see him through. It always had. He had patients to see on the wards, mounds of paperwork to wade through and departmental-sponsored research projects to figure out. The last thing he needed was to talk about his emotions.

John headed to the hospital and managed to do a quick ward round, pleased with the progress of his patients, without bumping into Mackenzie. He'd even asked the ward sister if Dr Fawles had been in this morning.

'Not yet, John, but we're expecting her soon.'

Relieved he'd missed bumping into her, still unsure what he was supposed to say to her, especially as he felt uncomfortable and embarrassed by his behaviour, John headed to his office with a couple of casenotes. As he walked, he flicked open the top folder and skimmed the patient's notes. It wasn't until he rounded a corner, not looking where he was going, that he realised that reading and walking weren't the best of companions.

'Whoa!'

John collided with someone, casenotes being knocked out of his hands, loose pages slipping from the file and falling to the floor. It wasn't until he'd automatically mumbled an apology, crouching down to gather up the mess, that he looked up to see just exactly who he'd bumped in to.

'Mackenzie!'

'John!'

'Er...' He frowned as he realised there were more sets of casenotes on the floor than he'd been carrying.

'Clumsy of me,' she instantly offered. 'I should know better than to read and walk, especially around this place.' Her smile was sweet, charming, and John felt the full effect in his gut.

'I think we're both to blame. Why don't you come to my office and we can sort out which bit of paper belongs with which set of casenotes?'

'Good idea.'

There was a slightly uncomfortable silence as they

walked along and Mackenzie was thankful the orthopaedic administration building wasn't too far from where they
were. She smiled at the admin staff as she followed him
into his office.

'Probably best if we don't put them on my desk. It's
still too messy.'

'Good idea. The carpet will be fine,' she replied, and
immediately sat down in the middle of his office floor,
crossing her legs and spreading the files out, picking up
the first of the loose sheets. 'Perhaps one day we will have
a paperless office,' she remarked, pleased when he joined
her on the floor. 'But it isn't today. Here. I think this blood-
test result belongs to one of your patients.'

They sat on his office floor, sorting things out, and
within a few minutes everything was shipshape again yet
John found he was in no rush to get to his feet. Now that
she was in front of him, his manners came to the fore and
he knew he needed to apologise for his behaviour the previous night.

'Listen, Mackenzie. About last night.'

'It's fine,' she interrupted. 'You don't have to explain
anything to me and I don't want you to think I was presumptuous before, leaving you with two voice-mail messages. Sorry about that.' Her words had tumbled out so
fast, almost tripping over each other.

'I didn't think you were being presumptuous. I appreciated hearing from you.'

'You did? Well...um...OK, then. Just...glad to know
you're...well...you know...OK.' Why on earth was she blath-
ering on like a complete twit? Mackenzie closed her eyes and
shook her head. Sitting here with him, crossed-legged in the
middle of his office floor, wasn't at all how she'd imagined
their next meeting.

Her heart rate had increased and her throat had gone

dry. What was it about this man that drove her completely ga-ga just from being close to him? Honestly, she was behaving like a hormonal teenager! She sighed, only then realising that neither of them had spoken for at least ten seconds.

Silence hung in the air between them and, starting to feel self-conscious and a little uncomfortable, Mackenzie racked her brains for something else to say. She wanted to ask him why, exactly, he'd bolted from her house but at the same time she didn't want to overstep the mark of this new friendship they were hopefully building. The fact that he'd gazed longingly into her eyes as though he'd like nothing more than to kiss her senseless meant nothing. Absolutely nothing.

'Er...Ruthie get off to school OK?' he asked, sounding as though he, too, was struggling to find a topic of conversation. He certainly seemed far more calm than he'd been when he'd rushed from her house.

'Yes. Yes. Friday mornings are relatively easy so we were able to take our time.'

'There are other mornings that are harder?'

'Yes. Ruthie has a violin lesson on Tuesday mornings before school and an extra reading class on Thursday mornings.' Talking about Ruthie was a safe topic and Mackenzie slowly began to relax a little, enjoying the sound of his voice as the deep resonance of his baritone washed over her.

'Violin lessons?' He grinned, imagining the scratchy, off-pitch sounds of a five-year-old playing a violin.

'It bleeds the ears but she enjoys it.'

John chuckled and Mackenzie instantly smiled. She'd managed to get Ruthie organised, drop her at school and have a shower. Thank goodness Ruthie had been content with her explanation last night when John had suddenly disappeared.

'He's a doctor, Ruthie. Remember?'

'Oh, yeah. Always working. Always busy. I get it.' She'd sung some of the words and wiggled her hips with a bit of attitude as she'd spoken, causing her mother to smile.

'So…' John continued a moment or two later, as though he was trying his best to ensure there weren't any more awkward silences between them. 'What happens when you're stuck at the hospital with an emergency? Who looks after Ruthie?'

'I have a good network of people around me more than willing to help out but, thankfully, I only work one on-call shift once every three months. It just makes it easier all round.'

'You always were a strong woman. I knew that from the moment I met you.'

'Really?'

'You'd managed to somehow get out of the car, move away from danger and find a safe place to rest. Not many women are that strong, Mackenzie. Not many women are that clear-headed in a crisis.'

'But I'm a trained doctor.'

'That was definitely to your advantage but over the years and throughout all my travels I've come across so many different people, in different circumstances and different levels of training, and yet none have affected or impressed me with their inner strength as much as you did during the time we spent together.'

Mackenzie was silent as he spoke, unable to believe he was saying such wonderful things. Tears of unbelievable happiness started to prick behind her eyes and she swallowed over the lump in her throat.

'Mackenzie?'

'Yes?' Her voice was soft.

'Are you…all right?'

'It's…um…been a very long time since someone told me they believed in me. Coming from a foster-home situation, always being put down, raised in a negative atmosphere and then marrying the wrong man doesn't do a lot for a person's confidence.'

'The wrong man? You mean Warick?'

'Of course, Warick.' She smiled. 'I've hardly had the time to finish my orthopaedic training and raise a daughter, let alone find another man, get married and divorced in five years.'

'Well, I don't know, Hollywood stars do it all the time,' he said lightly, and was pleased when she chuckled.

'Fair point.'

'So I take it your suspicions were confirmed? Was he having an affair?'

She laughed without humour. 'Judging by the four or so pretty paralegals who turned up at his funeral, all far more distraught than myself, I'd say that's a yes.'

'Four?'

'They were all quite open in their grief. Turns out Warick had never been faithful. Not even at the start of our marriage. I was merely a pretty possession he had to have. Brains and beauty. The perfect companion to help him rise in the legal profession.' She sighed. 'So you can see how sometimes, when people actually give me compliments and offer support, it's difficult for me to accept.'

'Did you believe me five years ago?'

'Yes, and that belief has helped me tremendously throughout the time since. I can't thank you enough, John. I don't think you have any idea just how much of an impact you've had on my life. You were there when I needed you most, and while I would have liked to stay in contact, to at least give you updates on Ruthie, I also accepted that you were my knight in shining armour, only there to rescue me when my need had been the greatest.'

It was probably the sweetest and most sincere thing anyone had ever said to him. 'It was my pleasure.' When he spoke, he was surprised to find his voice was a little husky. He cleared his throat and glanced away for a moment, sure that if he stared into her mesmerising eyes for much longer he wasn't going to be held responsible for his actions.

Mackenzie breathed in deeply, astonished to find a man who really was in touch with his feelings. Then again, he'd told her he'd been raised by older sisters so what did she expect? 'Anyway, before we turn this into the Mackenzie and John mutual admiration society, I'd better get going.' She tapped the casenotes in front of her as though to indicate she had work to do.

She stood up, gathering the notes in her arms, and smiled at him. 'I guess I'll see you in clinic this afternoon?'

John stood, too, leaving his sets of casenotes where they were. When he didn't immediately answer her, she shrugged one shoulder and turned towards the door. 'Actually…'

She stopped when he spoke and looked at him over her shoulder.

'Er…would you care to join me this morning? If you're free? I…er…have to lease a car and find somewhere to live and your knowledge of the local area would be a vast help.'

'Oh!' Mackenzie was clearly surprised at his request but couldn't help the wide and happy smile that spread across her lips. Now was her chance to give just a little bit of help back to John, to repay him for what he'd done for her in the past. Plus, how could she resist when he was all she could think about. John Watson was back in her life…and this time for much longer than a day and a half. John Watson.

Her knight in shining armour. *Her* John. The man who had believed in her.

'Or if you'd rather not…' he said quickly, when she didn't give a reply.

'I'd love to help you, if that's all right.'

John grinned from ear to ear. 'All right. So…'

'Meet you out the front in fifteen minutes?'

'Excellent.' He nodded, unable to believe how happy he felt at getting to spend the morning with Mackenzie. Moving forward with your life when you'd vowed to live in limbo wasn't easy but he also knew that spending time with Mackenzie would make him happy, and surely he deserved just a little bit of happiness?

CHAPTER SEVEN

'WELL THAT WAS fairly easy,' John remarked ninety minutes later as he and Mackenzie walked towards a nearby coffee shop.

'What? Hiring the car or stopping off to go crazy at the shopping centre? I think you bought something from every department.'

'Not the pet section,' he countered as they chose an alfresco table so they could sit in the sunshine. 'Yet.' He grinned at her as the waitress came and took their order.

'Are you planning on getting a pet?'

John shrugged. 'Why not?'

'Mr I-don't-like-to-put-down-roots?' She raised a sceptical eyebrow.

'I was thinking a nice goldfish in a bowl might do the trick.'

Mackenzie grinned, enjoying herself far more than she would have thought. After they'd left the hospital, Mackenzie laughing as he'd made a show of folding himself into her small car, she'd driven him to a car-hire office where, within the space of twenty minutes, he had himself a 'decent' car, as he'd termed it.

'At least I can drive without having to unhook my knees from my ears,' he'd teased. Next, he'd suggested heading to a shopping centre where he'd bought up big in sheets and towels, kitchen supplies and even some cushions, 'For when I hire some furniture,' he'd told her. 'After I find a place to live.'

And now, as he talked about getting a goldfish, Mackenzie had to put a clamp on her rising excitement at having John around and close by. His exit from her life, which had been as sudden as his entrance, had left her wondering for years what had happened to him. Several times, usually on the days when she simply hadn't been able to cope with her crazy, hectic world, she'd run searches on his name on the internet, but had only received information on research papers he'd co-authored. She'd read them all, wondering if their paths would ever cross again.

He was also, she'd belatedly realised, the man she now measured all others against. He'd been supportive, caring and thoughtful when she'd needed him most, and after experiencing such emotions she'd vowed never to settle for anything less. Then there had been the times when she'd woken up from a wonderful, beautiful, relaxing dream only to realise he'd been the star in all her fantasies. *Her* John. Her secret crush.

What worried her now, sitting across a café table from him and smiling back at him, was whether she'd built him up so much in her mind that the *real* John wouldn't live up to her expectations. She pushed those thoughts aside and decided to simply enjoy spending time with him, helping him. She shook her head, her smile increasing. 'A goldfish isn't a pet, you ninny.'

John fixed her with a disbelieving stare. 'I think there are a lot of aquariumists out there who would disagree with you,' he said, waving one arm in the direction of the people walking down the street in front of them.

Mackenzie laughed. 'There's no such word as aquariumists.'

'Sure there is. I just made it up.'

'You can't just make up words.'

'Why not?'

She thought about this for a moment. 'Well, because…' She stopped and shrugged. 'I don't know, you just can't because I guess nobody would know what you're talking about.'

John leaned forward in his chair and winked at her. 'Exactly. Keep people guessing.'

'They'll think you've gone mad, which, I might point out, for the director of a hospital department might not be the best tack to take.'

'Worried I might get locked away in the psychiatric wards?'

'If you did, I'd visit you.'

John laughed. 'Good to know.' He sat looking into her mesmerising green eyes, her sunglasses on her head keeping her loose blonde locks back from her smiling face. Good heavens, the woman was stunning, and the more time he spent with her, the more warning signals went off in the back of his mind.

He watched as her gaze dipped to his mouth, the smile slowly starting to slip from her lips. The atmosphere around them became clouded with repressed sensual tension and John silently willed her to lean towards him, to close the distance between them.

When the waitress arrived with their drinks, he eased back in his chair, almost pleased with the interruption. Mackenzie wasn't the sort of woman to leap into something without figuring all the angles, especially after her own past experiences. She was cautious, careful and he appreciated those qualities.

He was the type of man to throw himself wholeheartedly into new projects, such as they'd experienced that morning with hiring the car and buying paraphernalia for his new place—wherever that might be. But Mackenzie wasn't a project. She wasn't the type of woman to enter into a short-term affair with no questions asked and then be more than content to say goodbye when it was time for him to move on. And he appreciated that, too.

'So what's next on the list? Place to live?' she asked as he sipped his coffee.

'Yes. Any suggestions?'

'Buying or renting?' She looked at him over the rim of her cup, more than a little interested in his answer.

John frowned. 'I'm not entirely sure.' At least, he *had* been sure he wanted to rent because when his contract was up in twelve months' time, he'd had every intention of moving on. That had been until he'd met Mackenzie again. 'Do you have something in mind?'

'I might. I'm presuming you want somewhere close to the hospital?'

'Within a reasonable distance. Now that I have transport, it's not that big a deal but neither do I want to spend hours in traffic every morning.'

Mackenzie nodded. 'Well, there's a townhouse in our cul-de-sac that's up for sale but it's been vacant for the past six months and the owners might be willing to rent it out rather than sell.'

John stared at her. 'Are you sure? You'd want to live next door to me?'

Mackenzie put her cup down and spread her hands wide, surprised to find them shaking a little. She quickly clasped them together. 'Well, it's close to the hospital, in a nice area and readily available. You could probably move in tomorrow if you wanted.'

'But you'd be OK living next door to me?' He leaned

forward in his seat again, resting his hands on the table, a fraction away from hers.

'Why wouldn't I want to live next door to a friend?' she countered. 'Plus, this way you can get to know the other people who live in the other townhouses and expand your circle of friends. You did say you like to meet new people.'

'Yes, I did,' he agreed, and quickly thought through what she was saying. Surely it couldn't do him any harm to at least look at the place. 'If I moved in, we might even be able to car-pool if we're on the same shift.' John instantly grinned. 'But we'll be taking my car. Now that I don't have to get into your little clown car, I won't.'

Mackenzie laughed and a wave of relief washed over her. John was here for twelve months. *Her* John. Who knew what might happen? Before she could process what this might mean, a loud scream pierced the air. Mackenzie and John turned to look where, at the next coffee shop, a mother was crouched on the ground next to her young son, who seemed to be shaking violently.

'Help! Help!' The urgency of the cries made them both spring up from their seats and rush over. Several people had stopped to look, concern on their faces. Mackenzie noticed one of the waitresses on the phone, her eyes as wide as saucers as she spoke quickly.

'Are you calling an ambulance?' Mackenzie called loudly, and the woman nodded as Mackenzie and John shifted tables and chairs out the way in order to get to the young boy. 'I'm a doctor. Let me through. I can help.' She made her way to the child and knelt down. The boy appeared to be around four years old and was thrashing around on the ground, his body convulsing with spasms. 'He's having a seizure,' Mackenzie stated firmly.

'Move everything away, out of his reach,' John ordered other people who were just standing there, staring, com-

pletely unsure what to do. He looked at one of the waitresses behind the counter. 'Medical kit?'

'Yes.'

'Get it, please.'

Mackenzie looked at the overwrought mother, who was
kneeling by her young son, her hands clasped at her chest,
her pallor as pale as a ghost's. 'Does he have any medica-
tion?' she asked.

'N-no. He's never…done anything like…' She stopped
as the boy's foot kicked over a half-empty cup someone
had left on the ground, the liquid contained inside flying
through the air and spraying a few bystanders.

'Hold him down,' someone instructed.

'Put your fingers in his mouth or he'll swallow his
tongue,' another suggested.

Mackenzie ignored them, rolling the boy onto his side
to protect his airway and keep it clear. 'What's his name?'
she asked.

'Perry,' his mother said on a sob. 'Is he going to be all
right? What's wrong with him?'

'Perry?' Mackenzie called, ignoring the rest of the
crowd. She could hear John keeping everyone at bay, taking control of the situation so she could focus on Perry.

'Perry?' she called again. 'Perry. It's OK. Everything's
going to be fine.' Her words were calm and controlled and
as she placed one gentle hand onto his shoulder, still soothing in her speech, she felt his little body start to calm. The
spasms took a short while to subside and by the time they
did, they could hear the sound of an ambulance siren heading in their direction.

'Wha-what…?' Perry tried to speak as his gaze slowly
began to focus on Mackenzie's face. When he didn't immediately recognise her, he began looking around fran-

tically for his mum, his lower lip beginning to wobble. 'Mummy? *Mummy?*'

Mackenzie looked across at Perry's mother, who seemed to be as stiff as a statue, completely frightened by what had transpired. 'You're fine, Perry. I'm a doctor. My name is Mackenzie. Mummy's right here,' she said, quickly pointing. Perry turned his head and upon seeing his mother sitting there, staring at him in shock, he immediately tried to sit up, but Mackenzie placed a hand on his arm to stop him.

'Just lie still for a moment, Perry.' Mackenzie looked up at John, who was just accepting the medical kit from the waitress, and inclined her head towards the stunned mother. Instantly, John knelt down beside the distraught parent and placed a reassuring hand on her shoulder.

'It's OK now. He's come out of it and he needs you.'

'What?' The woman turned worried and confused eyes in his direction and John directed her gaze towards her little son. As the mother focused, belatedly realising that Perry had stopped fitting and was looking up at her, she instantly started to cry as she bent to gather him close.

'Oh, Perry. Mummy was so worried.'

At seeing his mother crying, Perry's own tears started to flow and Mackenzie took the opportunity to reach for the medical kit and pull on a pair of gloves. Thankfully, the kit contained a penlight torch and she checked Perry's pupils, noting that they were equal and reacting to light. She also checked his mouth to ensure he hadn't accidentally bitten his tongue but there was no cause for concern.

As she took Perry's pulse, announcing it to be within normal parameters for someone who had just had a seizure, John stood.

'Good job, Dr Mackenzie,' he stated, giving her a quick wink and a smile before looking down the street. 'Ambulance is here. I'll go and guide them through.' With that, he headed off, leaving Mackenzie to wish he wouldn't wink at her in such a fashion as it caused a devastating effect on her equilibrium.

'Mummy? You're squashing me,' Perry said, his tears beginning to dry a little. The boy's mother apologised and loosened her hold.

'Is there anyone you want me to call? Someone who can meet you at the hospital?' Mackenzie asked as she pulled off her gloves, balled them together and put them into her pocket.

'My husband,' the woman said, and rattled off the phone number to Mackenzie. After the call was made, Mackenzie helped the woman to gather her things together as John led the paramedics towards them.

As they transferred Perry to the stretcher, the little boy looking tiny, Mackenzie explained to the mother about seizures, and although she couldn't say for certain what had caused it until scans had been taken of Perry's brain, the mother was certainly less fraught by the time they were safe inside the ambulance.

'Can you come to the hospital with us?' the mother begged. 'You were very good with Perry. Do you have children?'

Mackenzie glanced up at John. 'One. Just a little older than Perry.'

'Then you know what it's like. You can understand that when something is wrong with your child, you need people around you who you can trust.' She was clutching Mackenzie's arm, lines of worry, concern and fear etched on her face.

'Of course we'll meet you at the hospital,' John declared, his soothing voice filling the woman with reassurance. It was the same tone he'd used with Mackenzie all those years ago and as they stood side by side and watched the ambulance head back into the busy Maroochydore traffic, its sirens and lights flashing, Mackenzie couldn't help but slip her hand into John's and give it a little squeeze.

'You're very good at putting people at ease,' she told him. 'It's a gift, John.'

'I thought it was called having a good bedside manner,' he returned.

'Then yours is *very* good.'

A slow smile spread across his face, highlighting the gorgeousness that *was* John. They both stared at each other for a long moment. His gaze dipped to take in her parted lips, the tension between them increasing within a matter of seconds.

It was clear there was something very real building between them but what they should do about it and what it might mean were questions to which she had no idea where to find the answers.

John eventually cleared his throat. 'We'd best—'

'Go.' She nodded and for another moment neither of them moved, not wanting whatever it was that existed between them to end. Eventually, they came to their senses at the same moment and let go of each other's hands at the same time.

'Focus,' she heard him mutter, and she couldn't have agreed more.

By the weekend, John had taken possession of number one in her cul-de-sac. He'd hired furniture and was busy moving in, Mackenzie, Bergan and the Allingtons all pitching in to help their new neighbour. Ruthie kept running around the town-house, hooting and giggling at the echoes in some of the empty rooms. She helped by carrying small things such as cushions and books and other bits and bobs that wouldn't break if she accidentally dropped them.

They'd met Perry and his mother in Sunshine General's A and E department, where Mackenzie had introduced Perry to Bergan. After ordering scans of Perry's brain as well as blood tests, he'd been kept in overnight for observation, but at this stage there were still no obvious reason why the little boy had fitted.

'That poor mother,' Mackenzie had said to John before they'd left the hospital. 'Sometimes not knowing what's wrong or what caused it is worse.'

'At least their general practitioner can take it from here and chances are it's the first warning sign that something may go wrong in the future.'

'Still,' Mackenzie had sighed. 'He's just so…little. It makes me want to grab Ruthie and hold onto her for the rest of her life.'

John's jaw had clenched tightly at Mackenzie's words. 'I know the feeling.'

Mackenzie stood with her hands on her hips, surveying John's new lounge room. 'All you need to complete your new bookshelves are a few framed family photos and this room will look like it's been here for ever.'

'I don't have any family photographs.' His tone was brisk, distant and she immediately looked up at him, astonished to see him frowning.

'Um, I didn't mean anything by it, John. I was just making a comment,' she said quickly, wishing she'd thought more about his situation before she'd spoken out loud. 'It was more of a general decorating sort of comment. I didn't mean anything personal by—'

'It's fine,' he said, closing his eyes for a moment and shaking his head. 'I…overreacted.' Without another word he turned and walked out of the room, leaving Mackenzie kicking herself for being so insensitive. Although it did leave her with the question of *why* he didn't have any personal photographs. In fact, most of the things they'd shifted into the townhouse during the day were either newly bought or newly hired.

From what she understood, all he'd brought from the hotel had been a few suitcases full of clothes, but perhaps he wasn't the sort of man to need his memories wrapped up in a pretty frame.

In the evening John ordered take-away dinners for all his helpers, everyone sitting around his new dining table, enjoying a time of friendship.

'Thanks for a great evening,' Mackenzie said as she carried a tired Ruthie to the door.

'No. Thank you for helping.' He rested a hand on her upper arm and smiled. 'It's been an exhausting but good day.'

'That it has and it's completely tired Ruthie out, which is always an added bonus.' She shifted the little girl in her arms, Ruthie mumbling as she rested her head against her mother's shoulder and closed her eyes.

'Did you want me to carry her?'

'No. It's all right. I'll manage. She's just such a dead weight when she sleeps.'

'But we're neighbours now. It's what neighbours do.' Before she could say another word he'd effortlessly scooped Ruthie into his arms and was heading out of his front door. Mackenzie went ahead of him, opening doors and heading up to Ruthie's purple room, pulling back the light duvet in readiness.

John placed the little girl onto the bed and Mackenzie removed Ruthie's shoes, before standing back and looking down at her baby. 'Time has flown by so very fast,' she murmured. 'Some days it seems like just yesterday we were in the hospital in Sydney, waiting for news of her surgery.'

'Yes,' he agreed softly, and as they stood there, looking down at the sleeping child, it seemed the most natural thing in the world for John to put his arm around her shoulders. Mackenzie sighed and shifted a little closer to him, both of them remaining silent for a while, content just to watch Ruthie sleep.

'It must be so difficult for you, John. So many memories of Mune-hie.'

'Yes.' He nodded. 'But today's been good. It's been a long time since I've been around a child for any great stretch of time and today, watching Ruthie's excitement at the echoes of an empty house, it made me realise that Mune-hie not only gave us so much joy but we gave her joy in return.'

'Oh, yes. I have no doubt about that. You're wonderful with Ruthie, which tells me you were also a wonderful father.' She glanced up at him. 'Bad things sometimes happen to good people. There's no rhyme or reason why. They just do.' After another comfortable and companionable silence she asked softly, 'Do you want to talk about her? Because I'd love to get to know your daughter through your memories.'

John remained silent but she felt his hand on her shoulder tense for a moment before relaxing. When he spoke, his voice was barely audible as they stood there, watching her daughter sleep.

'Mune-hie loved to sing.' He breathed in deeply as though even those words had been difficult to speak out loud. 'Jacqueline loved to sing her to sleep every night with a Tarparniian lullaby, or at least the closest the Tarparnians can get to a lullaby, given their language is rather guttural. We didn't want her to forget her heritage.' He took another deep breath but this time Mackenzie could hear the smile in his voice.

'We taught her the usual nursery rhymes and after singing them to her once or twice, she knew all the words and would mimic us perfectly.' His smile broadened. 'By the time she was four she was giving us and our friends little singing concerts that used to last for at least fifteen minutes, sometimes longer, depending on how much we all clapped.'

Mackenzie chuckled at this. 'She sounds so delightful, John. A happy little songbird.'

'Yes.' He looked from the sleeping child to Mackenzie. Her face was hidden in the shadows of the room but he could see she was smiling.

'Thank you,' she whispered.

'No. Thank *you*. I don't talk about them much because it hurts.'

'Perhaps by sharing your memories of their lives, of the wonderful times you shared, it might help dull the pain you've been carrying around for so long.'

'Is that your prescription, Doctor?'

She chuckled. 'It is, and personally I'd love to hear about them. Good memories should always be treasured, and treasure means more if it's shared.'

'What about you? Do you have any good memories of Warick?'

Mackenzie sighed and angled her head towards Ruthie. 'I've been conscious of only telling Ruthie the good things about her dad and making sure she has a picture of him so she can know what he looked like,' she said, pointing at a small picture on Ruthie's bookshelf of Warick's smiling face looking back at them from a purple frame.

'I tell her little things like the way he could peel an apple in one long curly strip, usually directly into his mouth. Or the way he would wear different-coloured braces to work every day.' She shook her head in bemusement. 'Warick had at least fifty different pairs of braces and it wasn't even like he needed them to hold up his trousers. He just thought they looked good.'

'You don't miss him?'

Mackenzie sighed. 'No. Sometimes I miss…having someone, you know, the whole sole-parenting thing. At times I think it would be nice to be able to come home, share the domestic duties and then once Ruthie was in bed just to sit and talk quietly.' She shrugged one shoulder. 'But I guess I get that with my close friends, who are more like family, so I really shouldn't complain.'

'It doesn't sound like you're complaining,' he remarked, remembering all too clearly how exhausting parenting could be. John breathed in deeply, now becoming consciously aware of Mackenzie's sweet scent. Mackenzie herself was incredibly sweet but he couldn't believe the pressure he felt had been lifted from his heart just by sharing with her, and to have her share with him in return only made him like her even more.

He'd thoroughly enjoyed spending time with her today and although there had been plenty of other people around, John knew they should probably talk about whatever it was that existed between them…but not right now.

John gave her shoulder a little squeeze before dropping his arm back to his side, then, as though she could understand his unspoken communication, both of them turned and made their way out of Ruthie's room, the glow of the night-light guiding them back to the hallway.

They headed downstairs. 'Did you want a coffee? Or I can see if I can rustle up a decent cup of tea.'

'Any cup of tea is decent so long as it's not drunk out of plastic or polystyrene cups,' he stated as he headed towards the front door. 'Thanks, but I'd better go. I have a pile of work to catch up on before Monday morning's meetings.'

'How are you going with all the research proposals? Managed to get them all straight?'

'Yes. I think I've managed it so I shouldn't need any help with them. Also, thanks again for today.'

'It was fun.'

'It was.'

They stood at her front door, facing each other, unsure what to do next. Should they shake hands? Should he kiss her cheek? What about a friendly hug? Nothing seemed right and the longer he stood there, trying to figure out how to say goodbye to this most extraordinary woman, the deeper the tension that existed between them became.

They'd been given the opportunity to become friends and today had been a definite step in the right direction. She was a special lady and deserved to be treated with the utmost respect and care.

'Well…' John reached for her hand and brought it to his lips, pressing a chaste but gentlemanly kiss to the knuckles. 'Thank you again for everything, Mackenzie.' He worked hard to ignore the quick intake of breath as his lips made contact with her skin. 'Sweet dreams.'

Without another word he turned and headed out of her front door, disappearing beyond the reach of her security sensor light into the darkness of night.

Mackenzie quickly closed the door and sank down onto a chair before her knees gave way completely. Did the man have any idea how he affected her? How on earth was she supposed to sleep now? And if she did, she knew exactly who those sweet dreams would be about.

CHAPTER EIGHT

MACKENZIE HARDLY SAW John at the hospital on Monday as she had an elective operating list in the morning and he had a string of back-to-back meetings. On Tuesday, they were in clinic together, both in professional mode, conferring together on one or two patients. On Wednesday, she was heading back from the hospice, having just seen a few of her more elderly patients, when she heard someone call her name. She stopped and turned, a bright smile flooding her face as she saw John jogging towards her.

'Hi. Where are you coming from?'

'The labs. I thought the best way to wrap my head around which project belonged to which researcher was to go over there and introduce myself.'

'Ah. Good thinking. So you would have met Stan, Anna's husband.'

He frowned for a moment. 'Anna's the theatre nurse?'

'That's right,' she said as they started walking back towards the hospital, the dazzling Maroochydore sunshine warming them both.

'So Stan's her husband,' he said, as though making a mental note. 'I'm slowly starting to piece things together.'

'Actually, you and Stan would get along quite well. He likes going hiking and doing all that outdoorsy stuff that I remember you like.'

He gave her a quizzical smile. 'You remember that?'

'John, you were covered in dry mud when we met. You'd been caving, right?'

'And rock-climbing.'

'Well, Stan likes all that stuff, too.'

'"Stuff", eh? Anyway, where have you been?'

'Hospice.'

'Everything all right?'

'Mrs Pegg just had another set of X-rays taken because I had a hunch things just weren't right.'

'And?'

'I'm taking her back to Theatre tomorrow morn—' Mackenzie's words were drowned out by a loud yelp. 'What was that?' she asked, looking around.

John was also instantly alert. 'It came from over there.' He pointed towards a building opposite them.

'That's the female wards.' As they both looked at the building, their eyes widened in utter surprise.

'That's a—'

'Patient,' John finished for her, and he was right. A woman of about eighty years old, dressed only in her cotton nightie, had somehow found her way out onto the third-floor balcony, which was usually only used by staff, but that wasn't what was troubling them. The elderly woman was sitting up straight, seemingly perfectly happy, her legs dangling over the wide concrete railing.

A nurse was at the window, having just spotted her patient. It was the nurse who had screamed in fear. Now that the immediate shock was over, the nurse was opening the window further, leaning out to try and get her patient's attention, but the old lady either couldn't hear very well or she simply wasn't taking any notice.

'Oh, no.' Mackenzie rushed towards the building, looking around her, wondering what they could use on the ground to protect the patient in case she fell. The woman seemed to be balanced very precariously on the balcony railing yet at the same time seemed more than content to simply sit there.

What on earth was she doing? Perhaps she didn't have any idea where she really was. Dementia, whether due to Alzheimer's disease or repeated strokes, could play the most cruel and sometimes deadly tricks on the mind. The woman's mental state might be completely volatile or quite placid. Silently, Mackenzie hoped for the latter.

'There's nowhere soft for her to land.' Mackenzie spoke the words out loud as she continued to scan the concrete area below the balcony, trying to think and plan for the worst-case scenario. She needed to get mattresses brought out, but from where?

The nurse was at the door to the balcony but for some reason wasn't able to get out. Mackenzie couldn't see the balcony properly but she could hear the pounding as the nurse banged on the door, desperate to get to her patient. The elderly woman grinned secretly to herself, seemingly pleased with being so clever.

'Hello up there!' Mackenzie called, but received no answer. Either the woman couldn't hear her or else she chose to ignore her.

'Plan B,' John murmured.

'Plan B?' Mackenzie asked, turning to glance at John, but to her surprise found she was talking to thin air. John was no longer standing beside her but was instead running towards the outside of the building at a rate of knots.

Mackenzie watched in utter astonishment as John launched himself at the building, clinging to the drainpipe that ran the height of the building. As though he were a superhero, he scaled the pipe to the third floor with ease, yet he was still quite a way over from where the woman sat, legs dangling, sometimes swinging them to and fro. What was he going to do? How was he going to get to the woman?

Mackenzie's heart leaped into her throat and her jaw dropped in disbelief as she watched John use foot- and handholds in the building's old stone façade to pick his way across, his taut body spread out flat like an agile insect.

People were crowding around, hospital security was bursting into action, organising mattresses to be brought out in case the woman accidentally fell or, even worse, jumped. Someone else kept stating that the fire brigade had been notified and was on its way. Mackenzie's eyes, however, were trained on her knight in shining armour.

John continued to make his way across the building but when he accidentally slipped a little, his foothold not as secure as he'd initially thought, Mackenzie gasped out loud, clutching her hands to her chest. His near miss had made her heart pound faster but her breathing stilled as she continued to watch, feeling helpless and yet mesmerised by what was unfolding right before her eyes.

When he had almost reached the balcony, the woman looked across at him. Mackenzie could just make out her expression and it wasn't one of surprise. It was one of happiness. It was as though the old lady had always known that John would be coming for her. It was an odd moment because Mackenzie had thought John's presence might startle the woman so much she'd lose her balance.

It was clear the poor lady really had no idea of her actual surroundings and as she continued to watch John, her smile became a cheeky one.

'So you escaped, too,' she said to him, her words drifting down to those watching below. John didn't stop moving but instead reached for the balcony railing and hefted himself over in one simple and easy move. His agility wasn't in question, neither was his bravery, and Mackenzie let out the breath she'd been unconsciously holding until he was finally safe behind the balcony railing.

'I sure have.' He moved steadily but cautiously towards her. 'I'm John. What's your name?'

'Patty.'

'Nice to meet you, Patty.' John placed a firm hand on either side of Patty's waist. 'Why don't we go and sit down on the chairs over there? We can talk some more.'

'I wanted to smoke,' Patty confessed, then scowled. 'My parents don't let me smoke.' She shook her head. 'It's silly. My parents are so old-fashioned, so out of date.'

John's hands were still firmly on Patty's waist. 'Come and sit over here and tell me all about it,' he suggested, obviously wanting to get her down by her own will rather than forcibly removing her from the balcony.

Mackenzie watched as he charmed the woman, as he smiled and spoke softly to her. She knew exactly how Patty must feel, especially with those blue eyes fixed on her as though she was the only person in the world who mattered to him.

Mackenzie closed her eyes, seeing him looking at *her*, telling her everything would be OK, that he was there to help her. She'd felt so lost, so afraid, especially when Ruthie had been rushed into emergency surgery, and then, as though he'd been sent from heaven above, he had been there, reassuring her, supporting her.

'I knew a man called John once,' Patty was saying, obviously in no hurry to move. Mackenzie opened her eyes and strained to hear exactly what they were saying. 'Are you him?'

'I don't think so. I'm a different John.' He paused and looked into her leathery, wrinkled old face. 'Do you know,

Patty, you have the most amazing brown eyes. So deep, such a vibrant colour.'

Patty's smiled brightened at his words. 'You *are* my John. You always liked my eyes, remember? You can't fool me, Mr Smooth Talker,' she said, and Mackenzie kept her fingers crossed that John would be able to get Patty back safely over the rail before Patty clicked back into reality and the whole scenario was jeopardised.

'Why don't you put your arm around my shoulders and I'll help you to the chairs over there? We can sit and talk.'

Patty eyed him a little closer, indecision obviously warring within her. Then John leaned closer and whispered something in Patty's ear that not only left the woman chuckling but leaning back against him, her arms going round his neck with ease.

In another moment John had Patty up in his arms and back onto the balcony, where he disappeared from view. The people watching below started to clap. Mackenzie momentarily closed her eyes and hung her head in relief, the tension easing out of her at the positive outcome to such a sticky situation.

Heading into the old stone building, she quickly made her way to the ward, where she found the nursing staff tucking dear old Patty back into her bed, John still holding the woman's hand, talking softly, his deep voice warm and soothing.

Mackenzie sat on a chair in the corner of the private room, wanting to stay out of the way but also wanting to listen. He really did have a knack for putting other people at ease, a perfect bedside manner. Patiently she waited for him to finish and when Patty was finally asleep John let go of her hand and turned, astonished to find Mackenzie sitting there, patiently waiting for him.

'I didn't realise you were here.'

'I didn't want to intrude,' she said, and when he pointed to the door, indicating they should leave, Mackenzie nodded and both of them headed out but not before the nursing staff had heartily thanked the handsome orthopod.

'You were so great with Patty,' Mackenzie said as they walked along the hospital corridors back towards the orthopaedic department.

'Thanks.'

They continued in silence for a few minutes before Mackenzie almost exploded with curiosity. 'Aagh. I can't take it. I need to know.'

'Know…what?' he asked in a slight teasing tone. They headed into the orthopaedic department and went directly to his office, where Mackenzie shut the door behind her.

'Stop playing it so cool. I'm sure you can see I'm going slightly insane, wanting to know more. What on earth did you whisper to Patty in order to get her off that railing? Whatever you said, it seemed to clinch the deal as far as she was concerned. How do you do that? How do you know just what to say in order to garner complete trust from someone you've only just met?'

John stood before her, hands shoved into his pockets, a small smile still on his lips. He raised his eyebrows. 'I'd have thought you of all people would be able to answer that question.'

'Well, I know what you said to *me,* but Patty's a completely different kettle of fish.' Mackenzie paused for a moment, thinking back to when they'd first met. 'In actual fact, it wasn't so much what you said but how you said it, the tone of your voice, the expression in your eyes. In one instant you were able to get me to trust you completely.'

'Yes.'

'Do you simply say what you feel needs to be said or do you really believe what you're saying.'

'Why can't it be both?' Mackenzie frowned for a moment, processing his words. 'What was it I said to you to make you trust me so quickly?' he asked, his gaze intent on hers, his voice filled with that deep, abiding resonance that seemed to vibrate through her when he spoke.

'You told me everything would be OK but you said it with such conviction, as though you truly believed it, that you made *me* believe it.' Her words were soft.

'So what makes you think I said anything less to Patty,' he stated.

'John! Stop teasing me.'

He chuckled then shrugged. 'It was nothing magical. I simply told her that she was an incredible woman and that I'd love to sit and talk with her.' He shrugged as he spoke the words.

'And that's exactly what you did.' Mackenzie nodded. 'I'll bet you listened to her talk, encouraged her to talk, to help bring her troubles out into the open so she could relax her mind and get some rest, especially after such an exciting ordeal.'

'I also took the opportunity to remove the chair Patty had somehow wedged beneath the handle of the balcony door in order to let the nursing staff through.'

'I was wondering why they couldn't get out. The sly old dear. Did you find out why she was on the balcony? Why she'd gone out there in the first place?'

'To have a cigarette. She told me she was nineteen years old and that she was sick and tired of her parents not treating her as a grown-up.'

Mackenzie smiled sadly, her heart touched by the words. 'Poor Patty.'

'The mind is far more powerful than we realise,' he agreed. 'At least she's safe now.'

'Thanks to you.' Mackenzie's smile increased and the

effect caused his gut to tighten. She took a step towards him, effectively closing the distance between them. 'You're a remarkable man, John.'

She tenderly pushed back a lock of his hair that had fallen across his forehead, amazed at the fiery sparkles that burst to life within her body at the contact. 'You give an incredible amount to other people. You're considerate and generous.' She slid her hand down to rest on his shoulder, looking up into eyes she would never forget, eyes that had radiated that same security he'd just provided for Patty.

'Mackenzie?' There was a hint of warning mixed with a large dose of confusion in his voice.

'Don't you feel it, John? This crazy thing that exists between us?'

'I do. I do feel it, most keenly, but is it right to pursue it?'

She shrugged one delicate shoulder and edged a little closer. 'Is it right to ignore it?' She slowly shook her head. 'I've never felt anything like this before. It's…intense.'

'Powerful.'

'Raw.'

John dragged in a breath and slowly let it out as he rested one hand at her waist, delighting in being able to touch her. 'You are…incredible, Mackenzie. I—'

He stopped, gasping as he gazed at her beauty. He reached out and tenderly caressed her cheek. She was right. It *was* intense and as he looked down into her upturned face his gut tightened with repressed desire. 'You are… exquisite.' He rubbed his thumb gently across her lips, his body pulsing with compelling hunger as her lips parted, her expelled breath hot and moist against his thumb.

'John.' His name was a whispered caress on her lips and he wanted it.

He wanted her sweetness, her touch, her need. He could

feel it thrumming through her and somehow it had managed to transfer itself to him. Both of them had the same powerful, burning need, which was drawing them closer together, each one momentarily fighting, each one losing the battle. Nothing mattered. Nothing except giving in to the delight he knew both of them would feel the instant he pressed his mouth to hers.

John couldn't believe he was about to kiss Mackenzie. He felt as though he'd waited a very long time to finally end up here, with this most glorious woman in his arms. He lowered his head and delight surged through him at the way she sighed, her body leaning into his, her eyes closing.

The moment their mouths finally touched, after wanting and needing these sensations for so very long, she was sure they had the ability to stop time. Wave after wave of burning desire washed over her, each one more incredible than the last. The pressure of his mouth on hers, the thrumming through her ears as blood pumped faster around her body, the taste of him blending with her own need...

She'd dreamed about this moment, woken up in bed with thoughts so wild and vivid that she'd almost felt his touch on her mouth. Now she knew all of her dreams paled in comparison to the real John. Her heart was pounding frantically against her chest and her body seemed to have come to life in a way she hadn't known existed before now.

He was here. *Her* John was here, finally, at last, and as he slowly moved his mouth against hers, seeming to savour every exquisite moment, making her feel feminine, pretty and secure, Mackenzie's heart soared with happiness.

Slow and sweet and seductive. His mouth continued to cherish hers as though he was desperate to memorise every single contour, every curve, every taste of her. Finally, after years of wondering what it might be like to kiss her one day, to sample her luscious lips, to taste her, to tantalise her, to take whatever she'd willingly offer him, John realised he was ill prepared for the power of the sensations the two of them evoked in each other.

'Mackenzie,' he murmured, needing to be absolutely sure this was what she wanted.

'Shh. Just kiss me, John. *Please?*'

He followed her orders, desperate to keep a tight control over the powerful surge of desire flooding through him. She deserved gentleness, tenderness and faithfulness. There would be a time for hunger, for heat, for the frenzied desire he felt for her, but not now. It took all his strength and mental skill to ensure he kept the exploration of her mouth soft and sweet, delighting in every discovered nuance and contour.

'You are…perfect,' he whispered as he pressed small kisses to the corner of her mouth before working his way across her cheek and down towards her neck. She angled her head slightly, allowing him access. He closed his eyes, unable to believe how fortunate he was that she seemed to be on the same page as him, wanting him to kiss her as much as he wanted to kiss her.

'I didn't realise it until we met again but I've wanted to kiss you for so long, Mackenzie.' He pressed two more kisses to her neck then eased back slightly to look down into her upturned face. 'I'm sorry if that bothers you.'

'Why would it bother me?'

'Because five years ago you needed a supportive friend.'

'And that's exactly who you were for me.' She smiled up at him. 'We can't help the way we feel, John. It's there. It's real. We've both changed a lot during the last five years but I think the thing we're most concerned about is vulnerability. It's not easy for anyone to open themselves up to someone new, to share their insecurities, especially where the heart is concerned.'

John agreed. 'These overpowering emotions don't happen every day,' he stated, as though he was still trying to get his head around their present situation.

'I know it's probably not as easy for you to move on from your first marriage as it is for me, given your life with Jacqueline sounds like a very happy one,' she said slowly, gently running her fingers along his jawline. 'But time moves on, much as we may sometimes want it to stand still.'

John rested his forehead against hers. 'I come with baggage,' he told her.

'Don't we all?' she returned with a wide smile. 'I guess what I want to know, John, is whether or not you're happy to…not ignore this.'

He pondered her words for a moment before lifting his head and nodding, giving her a lopsided smile. 'I don't want to ignore this.'

Mackenzie sighed with relief. 'Good.'

'But before we go any further, I'd also like to tell you that there *was* a reason I didn't keep in contact with you all those years ago.'

'Oh? Because I've always wondered. I mean, I didn't expect you to be there every day but you could have left me with a phone number so I could at least…I don't know, send you a gift basket of fruit as a thank you?' Her words were teasing but John could hear the thread of confusion lying beneath.

'It's nothing sinister, I promise. It's simply that I thought you needed space to deal with the enormous changes in your life. You'd survived a car accident, given birth to a premature baby and your husband had passed away. That's huge, Mackenzie, and along with Ruthie's surgery, well, the last thing you probably wanted was me hanging around in the background, bringing more confusion into your life.'

'I don't think you would have brought confusion, John. You've experienced the loss of a spouse so you would have known what I was going through.'

'And that's *why* I needed to disappear, to leave you to your life. Although I found you attractive, you didn't need my extra baggage weighing you down.' He shrugged. 'I was just someone who was there when you needed them.'

She looked up at him. 'I need you now, John, but in a completely different way.'

His smile was instant as he lowered his head and pressed his lips to hers once more. 'Good.' He silenced any further chat with a kiss, Mackenzie slowly sighing against him, responding to the way he managed to set her on fire.

She'd always hoped it would be electrifying between them and it was. Now not only was her heart singing due to the delicate and tender way he was kissing her but also because it was possible, just possible, John might actually choose to stay, to put down permanent roots.

She focused on the way he was making her go weak at the knees with the way his tongue was tantalising her mouth, his teeth playfully nipping her lower lip, exciting her with the promise of a lot more to come. This was John. *Her* John. With the way he was ensuring she was safe and secure within his arms, she hoped with all her heart that she *would* be safe with him—for ever.

CHAPTER NINE

MACKENZIE AWOKE THE next morning to delicious dreams of John but this time the dreams of him holding her close and pressing his mouth to hers hadn't just been a dream any more. It had been real. Very real, and she sighed against the pillow, remembering the way his kisses had been filled with the promise of a perfect passion still to come.

His mouth had meshed perfectly with her own as though they had indeed been made for each other, but when she had tried to deepen the kiss, to open her mouth wider, to tease him by running the tip of her tongue along his lower lip, to nibble at the corner of his mouth, the heat pulsing through her starting to build to an out of control state, John had eased back.

'What's wrong?' she'd murmured, confused. Didn't he want her? Hadn't he been able to feel the passion surging through her? Was it not surging through him, too? She'd leaned in and kissed him again, her mouth open, her tongue slipping just inside his mouth. John had kissed her back for a whole fifteen seconds before his hands had somehow slid from her waist to her forearms and he'd gently eased her back. 'John?'

'Patience,' he'd whispered against her mouth as he'd pressed small petal-soft kisses to her lips.

'But…don't you want—?'

'With *you*? More than anything,' he'd answered before she'd been able to finish.

Hadn't he been able to see the passion flooding through her? The need to explore further, to discover more, to uncover the raw power that existed between them?

'But I also think it's vitally important that we take our time, that we slow things down.' As he'd spoken the words, his gaze had been locked onto her lips, his visual caress doing absolutely nothing to slow down the fierce and out-of-control pounding of her heart against her ribs.

Mackenzie had known he was right, that they both needed to take a breath, to allow their minds to clear from the haze of pleasure they'd created between them.

'I'd better go,' he'd said softly near her ear.

'I don't want you to.' Even after what he'd just said, Mackenzie hadn't been able to stop the words from springing forth from her lips. John's answer had been to take her hand in his and lead her towards the door.

'Well, we're both tied up until the weekend, so how are you fixed for Saturday?'

'Make me a worthwhile offer and I'll ensure I clear my schedule.' She'd smiled and John had been unable to resist putting his arms around her waist once more and leaning down to press his lips to hers.

'I'd better make it a good offer,' he'd teased, the undercurrent of desire still winding its way around them.

'What do you have in mind?'

'Well, as Ruthie will be around, I don't think we should contemplate what it is *I* have in mind,' he'd stated, wiggling his eyebrows suggestively, and Mackenzie's smile had increased.

'OK. So…?'

John had cleared his throat. 'Well, a patient told me about a wildlife park that's close by.'

Mackenzie had nodded. 'We know it well. We're members there because Ruthie adores the place. She's a nature girl.'

'It's a date, then. You…' He'd bent his head and brushed his lips over hers. 'And Ruthie…' Another kiss. 'And me.' This time when he'd lowered his head Mackenzie had slid her hands up his arms, lacing her fingers at the base of his neck and urging his head to stay where it was, his mouth creating havoc with her already overflowing senses.

John most certainly hadn't complained, his lips capturing hers once more in a powerful and possessive kiss. Mackenzie had melted into the embrace, loving the feel of him close, of his hands at her back, of his mouth on hers.

Sighing against the pillows, the morning sunlight now streaming into her bedroom, the smile on her face was as bright and as big as it had been last night. In John's arms. She was positive it was the one perfect place she'd been searching for all her life, the place that made her happier than she'd ever been in her life. John. She was meant to be with John.

With an excited laugh she opened her eyes and flung back the sheets, eager to get up, to get dressed and to get her date with John under way. An hour later, she was busy trying to tame Ruthie's riotous curls into a ponytail.

'I want my hair like yours, Mummy, then we'll be the same.' Ruthie giggled, pointing to her black boots, blue jeans and light red jumper, which was exactly what Mackenzie was wearing.

With their hair pulled back in the same style, Ruthie reached out and gave her mother a hug. Mackenzie accepted the embrace, picking the little girl up and smothering her neck with kisses. Ruthie squealed and giggled, the delightful sounds filling their little home with love.

When a brisk rat-a-tat-tat came at the front door, Ruthie

yelled, 'John!' at the top of her lungs, then scrambled from her mother's arms and raced off to open the door.

Feeling a little self-conscious, Mackenzie quickly went into the kitchen to ensure the cooler bag she'd packed with drinks, sandwiches and healthy snacks for Ruthie was ready to go.

'You sound happy this morning,' she heard John say a moment later. Ruthie was talking non-stop, telling him about everything they would be seeing today and what her favourite animals were and how she loved the butterfly house and a plethora of other things.

'Where's your mother?' John asked when Ruthie paused for half a second to take a breath and a few moments later John appeared at the entrance to the kitchen. 'Hi.'

Mackenzie wiped her hands on a teatowel and turned to face him, her smile displaying her nervousness. 'Hi.' She was completely unsure what to do next. Should she cross to his side and place a kiss on his cheek? On his lips? Should she even contemplate kissing him in front of Ruthie? She'd never really found herself in such a situation before and as she went to pick up the cooler bag, she realised her hands were trembling.

'Uh…Ruthie?' She focused on her daughter, needing to do something to help control the riot of emotions zipping through her due to John's tall, dark and handsome presence filling her small kitchen. He was dressed in a pair of runners, blue denim jeans and a white polo shirt, looking cool, calm and casual. His hair was still a little damp from his morning shower and his spicy scent was joyfully winding itself around her, causing a heady feeling of desire.

'Yes, Mummy?' Ruthie's answer snapped Mackenzie's attention back to her daughter and it was only then she realised she'd been openly staring at John, practically ogling him. She quickly closed her eyes for a moment but not before seeing the interested grin that had started to spread over his lips…lips that she now knew so well.

'Yes, Mummy?' Ruthie repeated, a hint of impatience in her tone.

'Er…go and get your hat, please.'

'Can I bring Zoe?'

Right at that moment Mackenzie didn't care whether Ruthie brought her entire collection of dolls, she just needed her daughter out of the room. 'Yes, you can bring Zoe.'

'Yay!' Ruthie ran upstairs, calling to her doll, 'Hey, Zoe, Mummy said you can come, too.'

'She's certainly full of beans,' John remarked as Mackenzie turned and started checking the cooler bag once again, needing to do something in the hope that the small task would help her control her nerves.

It didn't work, especially when she heard John move quietly towards her. When he placed a hand at her waist and eased her round to face him, she quickly clasped her hands together.

'Need any help?' His tone was deep, intimate and his gaze now rested on her lips as though he couldn't wait to taste them again. He reached out his hand, tenderly brushing her cheek with his thumb. She gasped at the touch, her lips parting as she stared into his hypnotic blue eyes.

'John?' she whispered, swallowing over the sudden dryness of her throat. 'I've never been—'

'Shh.' He angled his body closer, slowly bending his head, giving her every indication that he was about to kiss her. Her heart felt as though it was hammering out his name in Morse code as her eyelids fluttered closed, wanting to memorise and capture every sensation he was evoking within her.

Finally, he brushed a feather-light kiss over her lips.

'Good morning,' he murmured, his deep voice washing over her, causing tingles of delight to flood down her spine and then spread throughout her entire body.

'Morning.' She opened her eyes and looked longingly up at him, a small, shy smile touching her lips.

'I'm looking forward to today,' he told her as his gaze once more encompassed her delectable mouth.

'Me, too.'

'And me, too,' Ruthie said, obviously having overheard their words as she came carefully down the stairs, Zoe in her hands, both doll and little girl wearing their hats. Mackenzie immediately shifted away from John, hoping her daughter hadn't seen them standing so close. She wasn't ready to answer Ruthie's often blunt questions, especially if the topic was John Watson.

Mackenzie cleared her throat and re-zipped the cooler bag. 'OK, I think we're all going to have a lovely, friendly day. Now, where did I put my hat?'

'It's by the front door, Mummy,' Ruthie pointed out as Mackenzie picked up the cooler bag.

Immediately, John reached out and took it from her. 'I've got it.' He smiled before turning to wink at Ruthie. 'Let the lovely, *friendly* day begin,' he said, reserving a special smile for Mackenzie.

She was relieved he'd picked up on her message and as they placed Ruthie's car seat into the back seat of John's car, Mackenzie hoped that by the time they arrived at the wildlife park, her heart rate would have returned to normal, although with John's close proximity she doubted that would happen.

When they walked towards the entrance of the wildlife park, Ruthie insisted on holding both their hands, jumping and swinging in the air between them. Mackenzie looked across at John and was surprised to find him looking back at her, a bright, happy smile on his face. The fact that the three of them together looked like a normal, happy family hadn't escaped her notice.

It was a nice sensation and one she'd never had with Warick, who'd always declared himself too busy to spend much one-on-one time with her. Today, though, she could pretend that she, John and Ruthie were a little family, intent on enjoying the wildlife park together.

The weather was perfect, the sky nice and blue without a cloud in sight and, probably because of that, there was quite a crowd coming to see the animals. They rode the small model train around the park, Mackenzie laughing as John sat in the small space, his knees bent up near his ears.

'This is almost as bad as your car,' he teased, and Mackenzie laughed. Ruthie sat beside him, grinning and smiling and laughing. It had been a long time since Mackenzie had seen her this happy and the sight of John and her daughter looking at her with brightness in their eyes made her sigh with longing.

Was it possible that this dream had some sort of hope of coming true? Was this amazing connection she felt with John something that could bring him permanently into her life? The thought filled her with nervous apprehension and she quickly pushed the serious thoughts aside, intent on just making memories and enjoying the rest of the day.

Ruthie fed the rainbow lorikeets, quite a few of the bright-coloured birds landing on her head and arms and making her giggle. When they visited the snakes, Ruthie insisted that John carry her for protection. This he did without any qualms. At the crocodiles, Ruthie ended up on his shoulders, more than content to commandeer John's attention and time.

Throughout the day, Mackenzie took photographs,

knowing that if, for some reason she couldn't yet fathom, things didn't work out between herself and John, she could at least look back on this day with fond memories.

As they sat under the shade of an old gum tree, Mackenzie lay down and sighed, closing her eyes for a moment and drinking in the serenity. Other families were also picnicking around the place and she could hear childish laughter filling the air, murmured conversations, birds squawking, leaves rustling in the light breeze.

'She's certainly a good talker,' John remarked as he watched Ruthie playing not too far away with a few other children, bossing them around. Mackenzie laughed at the comment and the sound was like music to his ears. She deserved to laugh, to be happy.

'As in too much?' she asked. 'She usually talks a lot faster than she is today. Sometimes I think she does it because she's so eager to get her point across before anyone interrupts her.'

'I'm not objecting.' He grinned at her before taking off his sunglasses and meeting her gaze. 'Would you like to have more children?'

Mackenzie seemed surprised at the question but more surprised at the intensity she could see in his gaze. She had the feeling this was some sort of test, although she had no idea why. 'Possibly. It would depend if I...found the right person. I've already fallen pregnant by a man who only agreed to have children because his boss told him that a family man was considered to portray respectability.'

'Really?' John shook his head. 'Warick, God rest his soul, doesn't appear to have been too bright when it came to knowing what was important in this life.'

Mackenzie lifted herself up on one elbow and looked at John. 'To be fair, I don't think any of us do until it's too late. Although Warick and I may have had our difficulties, he didn't deserve to die.'

'Do any of us?' he asked softly.

'I guess not.'

'Do you miss him?'

'Not as much as I did at first but, then, I was not only a brand new mother to a sick baby in the neonate unit in Sydney but a grieving widow. Coping with sickness and grief aren't good combinations to experience together but over the years and especially once Ruthie was on the mend and turning into a gorgeous little person, I started to realise that my marriage had been held together with sticky tape and string.'

'I'm sorry to hear that, Mackenzie,' he stated, his tone earnest.

'Warick had never been very strong, or at least not as strong as I'd believed when we were first married. Having been raised in foster-care, I had to believe that I could cope with anything but I have to tell you, *that* belief was definitely put to the test.'

'How did you end up in foster-care?' he asked, hoping she wouldn't shut him down now. He had the feeling that she was more than happy to talk about Warick because John had been the one to tell her of her husband's death. But her life prior to the events that had first brought them into contact with each other was still a complete mystery to him.

Mackenzie sighed and levered herself up into a sitting position, glancing over to where Ruthie was playing to make sure she was out of earshot because this story was one Mackenzie didn't want her daughter to know about until she was an adult.

'Well...' She dragged in a breath then shook her head. 'I'll say it fast. My father, drunk and in a jealous rage, shot my mother and then turned the gun on himself. I was seven years old, was in my room asleep and didn't know anything about it until a policeman burst into my room. The neighbours had heard the shots and called the police.'

She picked up a dried leaf from the ground and began to break it apart with her fingers, unable to bring herself to check what John's expression might be like. Usually when people first heard her story they would feel sorry for her, especially adults, and she hated seeing that pitying look in their eyes.

'And there you have it. That's my sad little story. I went to live with my aunt for the next few years but by the time I was ten I was a little…unruly, shall we say, and my aunt couldn't cope with me so I ended up in the foster-care system.'

John was quiet for a moment or two, processing what she'd said. 'No wonder you're so strong.' When he'd eventually spoken, his deep tones had washed over her with a hint of pride. It wasn't the reaction she'd expected and she lifted confused eyes to meet his.

'Pardon?'

'From the first moment we met I've been impressed by you, by the way you somehow manage to haul yourself up, to get back on your feet and to keep on going. That's an amazing quality, Mackenzie.'

'Oh.' She actually felt a little self-conscious at his praise and wished she hadn't worn her hair back in a ponytail because right now she would have liked to use it as a veil to shield her from his probing eyes.

'I've always thought you somewhat remarkable and now I know for sure.' His blue eyes held an intensity she found difficult to ignore and instantly she felt the butterflies in her stomach take flight and her skin prickle with an awareness only John could evoke. He edged a little closer to her, leaning one hand near where she was sitting, angling his body towards hers. 'It certainly couldn't have been easy for you, going from one foster-home to the next and every time having the history of your past trotted out.'

'It wasn't.' She shook her head slowly. 'The adults may have looked at me with pity but the other foster-kids used it as an excuse to taunt me.'

'Really?' His frown was deep as he reached out and gently brushed the backs of his fingers over her cheek. 'Kids can be so horrible.'

'It was the way of the foster-system. Some kids had parents who were drunks or drug addicts and for their own protection they'd been put into the system. Other kids were just dumped, sometimes not even knowing who their parents were. Everyone had a reason for being in the system and the way people coped was to pick on each other.' She sighed, her smile a little melancholy. 'I guess in that way, perhaps it made us feel closer. We were all in the same ditch, suffering the consequences of other people's actions, coping any way we could.'

He nodded. 'No wonder you're so strong,' he repeated softly, intimately, and caressed her cheek once more, leaning in a little closer, their breaths mingling. 'I'm having a difficult time keeping my hands off you.' His words were barely above a whisper yet inside her head they were loud and clear, words she was delighted to hear. 'You have the most delectable mouth, Mackenzie, and now that I've kissed you, all I want to do is to repeat that action over and over.'

'OK,' she breathed. 'I'll let you.'

John's smile was slow and sensual and she couldn't help but let out an audible sigh as she decreased a few of the millimetres that currently existed between them. In the distance she was vaguely aware of the people around them but everything faded into the background when John looked at her the way he was now, as though she were the most precious woman in the world, that he wanted to be with her, to touch her, to kiss her.

'I'm glad to hear that.'

'I get so lost when you're near.'

'Lost?' He breathed in deeply as though needing to fill his lungs with her essence as he lightly grazed his cheek across hers, his lips brushing the briefest of kisses along the line of her jaw. To anyone else it would have appeared he was whispering something in her ear but to Mackenzie he was causing her entire being to flood with pure delight.

'I don't know...what to think. Nothing is...ahh...' She gasped when his teeth nipped lightly at her earlobe. 'Everything is...foggy.'

'Foggy?' John couldn't believe how responsive she was to his teasing touches and how she'd managed to fan the flames of the small fire that had been burning within him ever since he'd been allowed to kiss her. Didn't she have any idea just how much she twisted his gut into knots? How she somehow managed to penetrate all rational thought?

He was a man who prided himself on always being in control, always keeping others at a certain distance. It had been the best way, he'd found, to cope during the past eight years since he'd been plunged into his own personal ditch. If he didn't allow himself to care too deeply for others then he would never again run the risk of feeling such pain.

Yet here he was, not only infatuated with Mackenzie but enjoying every moment he spent with Ruthie, too. These two females had somehow managed to break through the barrier he'd carefully erected around himself and brick by brick they were making their way into the centre of his heart.

He should be far more concerned than he was, should

be doing everything he could to patch up that wall, to put a bit of distance between them, but when Mackenzie was near him, when she looked into his eyes as though he were the one man in the world who not only understood her but had the ability to make her feel soft and sweet and sensual, then how was he supposed to deny himself?

Foggy. She'd said that his nearness had made everything foggy for her and he had to admit the same thing was happening to him. Her supple skin was becoming addictive, as were her luscious lips…and the way she looked at him, her green eyes so vibrant yet with a hint of vulnerability beneath…well, it was enough to drive even the strongest man to distraction and right now, when he was this close to her, he was not a strong man. He was like putty in her hands and the realisation scared him.

CHAPTER TEN

'MUMMY! MUMMY! LOOK!' Ruthie's excited cries caused John to withdraw instantly and Mackenzie immediately turned her attention to her daughter. There Ruthie stood, with one of the wildlife park's tame macaws on a tree branch next to where she was playing. The bird wasn't too disturbed by her loud cries of glee and, indeed, quite a crowd was already starting to gather.

'Wow.' Mackenzie picked up her camera and stood, or at least tried to stand. Unfortunately, one of her legs had gone to sleep and she crumpled back to the ground, a laugh bubbling up to the surface.

'Oops,' John said, and quickly got to his feet, slipping one hand around her waist as he helped her up. 'Here. Lean on me.'

Even though he'd meant the words in relation to her 'dead' leg, Mackenzie hoped he'd meant them in a permanent sort of way. She'd leaned on this man once before and he'd supported her far more than she could ever have expected. He was strong, honest and trustworthy and yet time and time again she still felt as though there was so much about him she didn't know, that she might never get to know if John refused to trust her enough to really open up.

They headed towards where Ruthie was still smiling excitedly at the macaw, one of the wildlife park rangers sauntering over to give the gathered children and adults an informal chat about the gloriously colourful bird.

'Look, Mummy! Look, John!' Ruthie gazed happily at both of them, pointing to the bird, and Mackenzie quickly snapped some more photographs, highly conscious of John's arm still around her waist.

'It's OK. My leg's working now. Just a few pins and needles as the blood starts to flow properly again,' she told him.

'I'm glad to hear it,' he remarked, bending his head and murmuring close to her ear, causing goose-bumps to spread down her spine before covering her entire body. She looked up at him and John took the opportunity to brush a sneaky kiss across her lips before reluctantly releasing her from his hold.

The reward for his cheeky action was a quick gasp of surprised delight before she forced herself to focus on what was happening to Ruthie. The ranger had asked for a volunteer and, of course, Ruthie's hand had instantly shot into the air. She was now standing in front of the macaw, being offered the chance to reach out and touch his bright, smooth feathers.

Mackenzie took far too many photographs and both adults listened again and again to Ruthie's excited chatter of the event on the drive home.

'And then, when I had the seeds on my hand and he pecked it with his beak, it tickled, Mummy. It tickled, John.'

'So you've said,' Mackenzie remarked, wondering if she'd ever get Ruthie to bed after such an exhilarating and enjoyable day, but by the time they arrived back at the cul-de-sac she was beginning to yawn. John carried the bags inside and Mackenzie went to run Ruthie's bath. She returned to find John saying goodnight to Ruthie, who was still yawning.

'Wouldn't you like to stay for some dinner?' she offered, but he shook his head.

'I'd like to but I do have a lot of paperwork to get through.'

She nodded, knowing the story all too well. 'Just because the sun is setting, it doesn't mean the day has ended.'

'Right.'

Ruthie walked over to her mother, holding out her arms, and Mackenzie dutifully picked up her daughter, who rested her head on her mother's shoulder. 'Then I guess I'll see you…some time tomorrow? Ward round?' She couldn't help but gaze longingly at his lips, wishing she could have one more of his special, mind-numbing, knee-knocking kisses but with Ruthie close she didn't think it a good idea. John seemed to understand her look, a slow smile spreading across his lips as he winked at her.

'I guess you will.' He headed out of the front door then turned to wave. 'Sleep well. Dream sweet.' As he walked next door, Mackenzie couldn't help but wonder if he'd really meant, *Sleep well, dream of me,* because that was certainly the subliminal message she'd been sent…and who was she to argue?

On Monday night, after a busy day at the hospital, Mackenzie headed to Grandma Liz's day-care to collect Ruthie.

'John's not here *again*?' the child protested as she climbed into the back of her mother's car.

'He's only come to pick you up once, Ruthie, and that was a special occasion.'

'But I *liked* it.'

'Well, he was still at the hospital when I left,' she told

her daughter, but by the time they pulled into the cul-de-sac John's leased car was parked in his garage.

'Can I go and say hello?' Ruthie asked eagerly, her eyes glittering with anticipated excitement.

'John may have a lot of work to do.' Mackenzie garaged her car, a little unsure what the protocol was now. Were they dating? Were they considered an item? Could she just drop round or call him up whenever she felt like it?

Even today, after she'd finished an elective theatre list, Anna had caught her standing in the change rooms, smiling secretly to herself as she'd thought about the way John kissed her so completely she forgot everything.

'You're in a good mood,' Anna had pointed out. The theatre nurse had eyed Mackenzie closely, before raising her eyebrows in surprise. 'And it seems to be something romantic that's put you in such a frame of mind.' She raised a finger to her lips and tapped it thoughtfully. 'It couldn't possibly be the new orthopaedic boss, eh? I heard what he did to rescue that elderly woman. He's a regular superhero, scaling tall buildings in a single scramble.' Anna had chuckled. 'Everyone's talking about it.'

'He really was quite amazing.' Mackenzie had smiled, shrugged and continued to brush her hair before pulling it back into a plait. 'Actually, John met your husband the other day when he was over at the labs, introducing himself to all the researchers. I told John that Stan also likes to go caving and hiking and do all that type of adventurer stuff. Perhaps the next time Stan's heading out, John could go with him.'

Anna had nodded. 'Sounds good. He's actually taken the afternoon off and is out at the national park, doing a bit of climbing. He says it de-stresses him.' She'd smiled fondly as she thought of her husband. 'I'll be sure to let him know about John's interest.'

'Thanks. John doesn't know very many people here in Maroochydore so that would be nice.' At her words Anna's eyebrows had once more hit her hairline.

'Are you the new boss's social director?' The theatre nurse had laughed at her own joke.

'No, but I do know what it's like to move to a new city.'

'And you're determined to help him settle in, are you? Well, it's about time a man grabbed your attention. He's a handsome one, too, *and* a superhero.'

'And my neighbour,' Mackenzie had admitted as she'd finished changing. She'd checked her watch, then gasped. 'Oops. Gotta run or I'll be late for Ruthie.'

'Wait,' Anna had called as Mackenzie had headed to the door. 'You can't drop a bombshell like that and not give me any information!' Mackenzie had chuckled and blown her friend a kiss before leaving the change rooms.

Now, after corralling her daughter inside and getting her into a nice warm bath, Mackenzie set about preparing dinner, telling herself to stop thinking about the man who was so close yet so far. So they'd kissed. So they'd admitted a mutual attraction. So they'd had a wonderful day together at the wildlife park. That didn't mean they needed to immediately start living in each other's pockets.

Perhaps she should invite him round for dinner? No. She didn't want to appear too needy. She'd told him when they'd first met again that she didn't have time in her life for romantic entanglements and it was true. Ruthie, work and home took up the majority of her time and what was left over she spent with her friends.

'Isn't John your friend?' she whispered as she put a pot of potatoes on to boil. It was only a meal…and they both had to eat…so they could eat together… She walked to her phone and put his number in but didn't connect the call. Instead, she shook her head and cancelled the call. He *did* have a lot of work to do and the last thing she wanted was for him to think she was crowding him.

Mackenzie stirred the pot of goulash before chopping up some more vegetables. She was an independent, self-sufficient woman who had survived for several years on her own. She and Ruthie were doing just fine and she most certainly didn't need a man to complete her life.

She rested her knife on the chopping board and looked towards her phone at the other end of the bench. Ever since he'd come back into her life she'd been a mass of confusion, wondering what might happen between them. She'd always been so cautious about any sort of relationship, having seen some terrible things when she'd been in the foster-care system.

When Warick had started to court her, she'd made him work hard to earn her trust. It had been such a blow when she'd eventually discovered their relationship hadn't meant anything to him. She'd just been a possession. And now she had Ruthie to consider as well. Her daughter was already far too attached to John and that caused her concern. If, for some reason, things didn't work out between them, how was Ruthie going to cope?

No. It was better that she leave things alone for this evening. John could stay at his place and do...whatever it was he was doing, and she and Ruthie would have dinner, watch a bit of television and then it would be time for homework checking, brushing teeth and story time snuggled up in Ruthie's purple bed. Definitely the best option.

'Mu-mmy!' Ruthie's sing-song call came from the bathroom at the same time that Mackenzie's phone buzzed to life and the doorbell rang.

'Oi with the poodles! If it doesn't rain, it pours.' She quickly wiped her hands on a towel, trying to figure out which to handle first. 'Just a minute,' she called to both

Ruthie and whoever was at the door. She answered her phone as she walked to the front door. It was Bergan. 'Hi, Bergan. Just a minute.'

'Mummy, I'm ready to get out!' Ruthie called again, this time much louder, just as Mackenzie opened the front door to find John standing there with a loaf of continental bread and a bottle of wine.

'Hi,' he said with a bright smile. 'I could smell whatever it is you're cooking from my place and thought, hey, why don't I just invite myself over?'

'Mummy!' Ruthie's impatience was starting to increase.

'Mackenzie?' Bergan said in her ear.

'Hi, John.' She motioned for him to come in. 'Sorry, Bergan. What's up?'

'Sorry,' John said, belatedly realising she was on the phone.

'Emergency,' Bergan replied. 'Did I just hear you say John's name?'

'Yes. He's here.' Mackenzie locked eyes with John and mouthed the word 'Emergency'. John rolled his eyes. 'What's going on?' she asked.

'A person has fallen down a cliff at the national park,' Bergan informed her. 'The rangers have called it in but we'll need a retrieval team. I'll need both you and John.'

'OK, Bergan. Is there a list of injuries?'

'Mummy!' Ruthie was starting to get angry now.

'I'll get Ruthie,' John said, placing the bread and wine on the coffee table and walking through Mackenzie's house. She closed the front door and turned to watch him disappearing into the stairwell as she listened with half an ear to what Bergan was saying. John was so relaxed and comfortable in her home, pitching in to help, tending her child. It felt odd. It felt strange. It felt…right.

* * *

Twenty minutes later John and Mackenzie pulled up in John's car into Sunshine General Hospital's car park and headed inside to the A and E department. Mackenzie had been stunned at how much easier it had been having John around to help with getting Ruthie organised.

By the time she'd finished the call from Bergan, John had scooped Ruthie out of the bath, wrapped her in a big, fluffy purple towel and carried her to the purple bedroom. While Mackenzie had dried and dressed her daughter, John had gone down to the kitchen, switched off the pots and made a few strawberry jam sandwiches for Ruthie.

'I wasn't sure where you'd be taking her but figured she'd at least need *something* to eat,' he'd told her when she'd thanked him for his thoughtfulness. 'And the Allingtons don't mind looking after Ruthie when emergencies like this happen?'

'No,' she'd told him. 'They're both retired medicos and two of their children are doctors so they understand what it's like. I'm incredibly lucky to have such supportive people around me.'

'I think it's because you give support in return.' He'd taken her hand in his and given it a little squeeze.

'I...uh...don't see that,' she'd murmured, hot tingles of excitement shooting up her arm before bursting throughout her entire body at his touch.

'Really? How long have you been friends with Bergan? I remember meeting her in Sydney so it has to be well over five years.'

'Bergan's different. We're foster-sisters and she was the one who supported me. She's a year older than me and back when we were sixteen and seventeen, that age difference was a lot. She was determined to get out of the hole she'd been in all her life.

'Once we even ran away from our abusive foster home.'

John raised his eyebrows at this news and Mackenzie nodded.

'It's true. We made our way to the Gold Coast, here in Queensland and lived on the streets for about six months. It was tough and sometimes we weren't sure where our next meal was coming from but then Bergan learned that as we were both registered in the foster system, that the government would subsidise our medical degrees.' She spread her arms wide. 'So that's what we did. We returned to New South Wales and started our training. Bergan had always looked out for me. She was my hero and she would always tell me that I was intelligent and could do anything I wanted if I just focused and worked hard, and she was right. But she gave to me, I didn't give to her.'

'I think Bergan would see it very differently.' He'd smiled and given her hand one last squeeze before returning it to the wheel. He hadn't been surprised she had low self-esteem. From what he'd seen during his time working in Australia and even in the UK, being a part of the foster system wasn't the most uplifting experience, but Mackenzie had already overcome so much, achieved so much and now was it any wonder that when she asked for help, the people in her life were only too willing to provide it? He'd seen the bright, beaming smile on Mrs Allington's face when Mackenzie had taken Ruthie over.

'Her bed's all ready. We'll play some games and then read some stories.' She'd clapped her hands and so had Ruthie. 'It's going to be as much fun as it always is.'

As they stood in the A and E department with the other assembling members of the retrieval team, waiting for Bergan to finish a phone call, John watched as Mackenzie interacted with her colleagues. She was highly intelligent, personable and incredibly pretty. He was sure she didn't see herself in such a way and he decided it was up to him to convince her of just how wonderful she really was.

Mackenzie turned and caught him staring at her but instead of looking away he held her gaze. He'd been watching her. The realisation washed over her with a warm flood of anticipatory delight. He really was interested in her and the knowledge made her feel quite light-headed.

It wasn't until Bergan had finished her phone conversation and called for their attention that Mackenzie broke her gaze from his, needing to reach out a hand to a nearby chair for a bit of support due to her less than stable knees. Good heavens, the man was enigmatic.

'OK, people. Listen up,' Bergan said. 'I have more information from the rangers out at the national park and I'm sorry to say that our patient...is one of our own.' She definitely had everyone's attention now. 'Stan Greggorio.'

There was a collective gasp. 'Has someone contacted Anna?' Mackenzie asked.

'Anna and her boys are on their way in now.'

'She told me he was going out this afternoon to do some climbing.' Mackenzie shook her head in stunned amazement. 'Poor Stan.'

'Yes, but we're going to be helping him out. One of the park rangers will meet us all in the main car park,' Bergan said, her tone brisk and commanding. She pointed to an image of the national park on the computer monitor. 'The rangers say that Stan is in this area, so we'll need to hike to get there. The rangers are setting up lights as the retrieval won't be complete before the sun sets. Now, as Stan has taken a tumble down a small cliff face, John, as our new orthopaedic director, it's time for you to earn your stripes.'

'Looking forward to it,' he said with a nod.

'Good. Mackenzie will abseil down with you. The two of you will stabilise Stan and get him ready to be transferred to the top, where Katrina and I will take over.' Bergan continued with her plan but Mackenzie had made the mistake of looking at John, who had winked at her, causing her insides to turn to mush. It was the last thing she needed and when she finally returned her attention to what Bergan was saying it was to find her friend giving her a dirty look.

'You couldn't stop flirting with him, Mackenzie,' Bergan growled at her once she'd finished her briefing and everyone had been dismissed to make their final preparations. 'A part of me simply didn't appreciate it while the other part was secretly jumping for joy.'

'What? Why?'

Bergan's smile was wide. 'I know John was there for you all those years ago and that you were upset when he left so suddenly, especially after helping you through such a difficult time, but, sweetheart, you need to control your expressive eyes whenever you look at him.'

Mackenzie raised her hands to her cheeks, realising they did feel rather warm. 'Am I blushing?' she whispered, and Bergan nodded. 'Oh, no.'

'I presume you came in the same car? And what was he doing at your place when I called, eh?' Bergan waggled her eyebrows up and down in a suggestive manner.

'Hey! You shouldn't be teasing me, you should be getting ready to lead this retrieval team,' Mackenzie complained, trying desperately to shift Bergan's attention from her.

Bergan only grinned, flicking her long auburn plait back over her shoulder. 'I'm brilliant at multi-tasking. You know that.' Bergan hugged her friend close. 'Be careful, little sis,' she whispered in her ear, then pulled back. 'Oh. Anna's here.' The smile slid from her face.

'Let's go and speak to her.'

John watched as both Mackenzie and Bergan went to

reassure the theatre nurse, hugging their friend close and providing her with all the information they had. Anna's teenage boys were in shock at the news but Mackenzie gave each of them a hug, talking to them and making sure they weren't brushed aside through any of this.

She cared so much about others, a quality he admired and appreciated. Yes, helping Mackenzie Fawles to realise how amazing she was had definitely become his new goal. He grinned to himself. It was a tough job, but someone had to do it.

They headed out to the national park in one of the hospital's mini-vans, John more than happy to sit nice and close next to Mackenzie.

'How's Anna holding up?' he asked her, and she turned to look at him, which she realised belatedly was a big mistake. They were sitting so close, their scents mingling to form a heady combination, causing her mind to go blank.

'Er...she's, um...' Mackenzie's gaze momentarily flicked down to his lips before she cleared her throat and looked him in the eye once more. 'Doing as well as can be expected. Naturally she wanted to come out with us but Bergan managed to talk her out of it.'

'She wouldn't be able to remain detached.' John's words were clear but soft, his deep voice causing a thrill of excitement to flow through her. The tension between them was increasing the more time they spent together, whether it was at work or not. When she looked at him like that, her eyes bright and shining with pure heart-warming emotion such as he'd never felt before, John wanted nothing more than to put his arms about her shoulders, draw her close and capture her perfect mouth with his own.

The intensity of the response she was able to generate within him was more powerful than any adrenaline rush he'd ever encountered during all the extreme sports he'd done over the years. She was taking him to new heights and he was beginning to experience an emotional terrain he'd never thought he'd go through again.

'I want to kiss you. Now,' he growled, his tone intimate, his back ramrod straight, every muscle in his body taut from resisting the urge.

'Music to my ears,' she teased, and he shook his head.

'How can you do that to me?'

'What?'

'Make me feel so powerful yet completely lost at the same time. Honestly, Mackenzie, you muddle my thinking.'

'I do?' Her smile slowly faded as she looked into his eyes, the tension surging between them far too intense for the likes of a crowded mini-van filled with other colleagues. 'Sorry.'

He slowly shook his head, brushing the backs of his fingers over her cheek. 'Don't ever think you have to apologise for making me feel this way. I like it, Mackenzie. I like it a lot.' He continued to stare into her eyes for a moment longer before the mini-van hit a pothole, jolting them in their seats and snapping them back to reality.

John cleared his throat and Mackenzie shifted, trying to put a bit of distance between his warm, firm thigh and hers.

'Focus,' he grumbled, more to himself than to her.

'Good idea,' she returned, as the mini-van slowed down to enter the car park. They all climbed out and were met by one of the rangers—Ted. He gave them all a quick debrief of the area through which they'd be hiking, telling them to bring with them whatever equipment they might require.

'How long will it take to get there?' Bergan asked, completely focused on the retrieval.

'About fifteen to twenty minutes. We follow a path for the first five minutes but after that the ground is rather uneven so please remain alert.'

Ted was right and not long after they left the path, everyone busy concentrating on where they were putting their feet. Mackenzie and John held back and brought up the rear of the group. As they traversed a rocky hill, Mackenzie noted that John seemed as comfortable with the terrain as a mountain goat, stepping with ease and confidence while the rest of them remained cautious and tentative.

'You really like your outdoorsy stuff, don't you,' she stated rhetorically.

He nodded. 'I do. No matter where I go, there are always new mountains, new amazing sights, new challenges.'

'How long have you enjoyed this sort of thing?'

'From my teens and especially once my parents passed away. I was a late-in-life addition to my family and, as I think I've mentioned, my sisters are much older than me. Hiking, caving, abseiling, anything I could do outdoors was done without one of them looking over my shoulder.'

She nodded. 'Like a release from the pressures of everyday life.'

'Exactly.'

'I was like that with reading. Easy to lose myself in a book.'

He shook his head, realising there was still so much about her he didn't know. 'Any particular favourites?'

She smiled. 'Too hard to choose just one.' Mackenzie paused for a moment, wanting to ask him a very personal question but unsure how he'd take it. 'I'm presuming you also hiked and rock-climbed a lot after your family passed away?'

John glanced her way, noting the slight dip in her tone and seeing the open concern in her eyes. 'Yes. Getting back to nature, seeing the untouched beauty…well, it definitely helped with the healing process.'

'I'm glad, John.'

He reached out with his free hand and gently touched her fingers. 'So does talking about it with someone who is willing to listen.'

Mackenzie was touched by his words and gave him a small, shy smile. 'Any time.'

'Hey!' Bergan called from the front of the group as she glared back at the two of them. 'Will you two stop lagging behind, please?'

Mackenzie and John instantly grinned at each other. 'Sorry,' Mackenzie called as they quickly picked up their pace.

They were all already dressed in the yellow and blue A and E retrieval overalls and when they arrived at the site they found that their ranger guides had brought several abseiling harnesses out with the rest of the equipment. As the sun was almost down, lights had been set up in the area as well as helmets with torches attached, ropes and other equipment they'd require.

'Gordon? Do you read?' Ted, who had been their guide so far, was saying into his walkie-talkie.

'Read you loud and clear,' came back Gordon's voice. 'You in position?'

'Just arrived. How's the patient?'

'We haven't been able to get to him yet. We've just finished clearing the side of the cliff to allow effective retrieval, so your timing is good. Are the docs ready to come down?'

'They're getting into harnesses now,' Ted stated, and continued talking to his colleague as Mackenzie and John slipped into the abseiling harnesses.

'Have you ever abseiled before?' John asked as his deft

fingers clipped and buckled things into place. Mackenzie was still turning her harness round, having already put her foot through the wrong hole once.

'Yes. I've been trained and out on retrieval several times and I'm quite fine once I have the harness on, but—'

'Here,' John said, grinning from ear to ear as he took the harness from her and held it out so she could step into it. 'Let me help you slip into something uncomfortable.' His tone was teasing and she couldn't help but smile up at him.

'Don't tease me. I'm trying to keep my thoughts focused.'

'Me? Tease?' His clever hands were moving around the harness, ensuring she was clipped and buckled in safely. 'Never!' He reached for the abseiling ropes, pleased he had the opportunity to hook Mackenzie in, ensuring it was done correctly. He was sure ranger Ted was good at his job but this way John *knew* Mackenzie was as safe as she could be in the circumstances, and the knowledge was definitely paramount to his own peace of mind. Next, he picked up a helmet and put it on her head. 'A definite fashion look,' he murmured, and switched on the helmet light.

'Well, you'd know, given you're such a fashionista,' she bantered back lightly as she picked up one of the portable medical kits they'd carried down with them and attached it to her retrieval suit. John's answer was a low, deep chuckle, which had the ability to set her entire body alight.

'Could you two stop flirting long enough to be ready to go?' Bergan asked coming over to them.

'Ready and raring.' Mackenzie couldn't believe the adrenaline pumping through her. John's answer was a firm nod before he walked towards the edge of the rock face.

As Mackenzie and Bergan watched, he lay down and peered over the edge, studying the layout below. His movements were sure and confident but even seeing him lying that close to the edge turned Mackenzie's stomach and her new-found nerve momentarily fled. If John were to fall…

'He really is confident around the edge of that cliff,' Bergan commented, both of them watching John.

'Yes, and he's scaring the life out of me.'

'Your own knight in shining armour in the flesh.' Bergan shook her head in wonderment. 'You deserve the world of happiness, Mackenzie.' They watched as John rose to his feet and started chatting with Ted, clearly wanting as much information as possible.

Bergan looked at her friend, her words heartfelt and sincere. 'And if he's the man to give it to you, then go for it.'

Was he the man to provide her with a lifetime of happiness? Mackenzie wondered. Would he leave at the end of his contract at Sunshine General? Continue his roaming existence? He'd already walked out of Ruthie's room, unable to deal with the rush of emotions from his own past, but he had opened up a little since then and talked about his family. Surely that was a good sign that he was starting to change his ways?

Mackenzie shook her head and even though her feet were presently on firm and solid ground, on an emotional level she felt as though she were about to tumble headlong over the cliff of love.

CHAPTER ELEVEN

JOHN MOTIONED MACKENZIE over to the edge of the cliff.

'Time to go?' she asked him, feeling more confident with what they were about to do because of John's strong and commanding presence.

'Let me check your ropes,' Ted said, but John stepped in front of the ranger before he reached Mackenzie.

'I've got it,' John said as he checked Mackenzie's clips and clamps one more time. Ted watched his deft fingers and nodded once the check was done.

'Right. You're both good to go.' Ted held the walkie-talkie to his lips and spoke to Gordon. 'Two docs coming over.'

'Belay in position,' Gordon called back.

'Ready?' John asked Mackenzie, and it was only when she looked into his gorgeous eyes, knowing she could trust him for ever, that any nerves or qualms she might have had vanished.

'Ready,' she replied.

'I'll go first. You follow.'

'Good.'

With that, John shifted to the edge of the cliff, turned his back on the drop and with a brief wink in her direction jumped backwards off the cliff, disappearing instantly out of sight.

'You're next.' Ted motioned to Mackenzie.

'Um…I think I'll take a more slowly-slowly approach,' she said, and after taking a breath turned her back to the drop and carefully leaned back in the harness until it was taking her weight. With gloved hands firmly on the rope, she edged over the cliff face, feeding the rope through with her hands. Once she was over, she slowly let the rope out, sliding herself carefully down the drop.

'Almost there,' John called. 'Excellent.'

In the next instant she felt his hands at her feet then they slid up to her waist as he pulled her onto the small ledge. Gordon was further below them, controlling the abseiling ropes. 'She's down,' John called, and within a moment Gordon had relayed that information up to Ted.

Now safe on the ledge, Mackenzie turned her attention to the job at hand and looked at the supine patient, who John had quickly wrapped in a space blanket in order to keep him warm. 'Let's see how Stan is,' she said as she pulled off the abseiling gloves, unclipped her medical kit and slipped her hands into a pair of medical gloves. 'Stan? Stan? It's Mackenzie. Can you hear me?'

She received no reply. John clipped a stethoscope into his ears. 'Airways are clear. He's obviously knocked himself out so…' John took off the stethoscope and felt the back of Stan's head with his gloved hands. 'Ah, yes, cranial fracture.'

Mackenzie angled the light from her helmet onto Stan's face. 'There's blood around the base of his neck so, yes.' She pulled out a bandage pad and took the wrapper off, handing it to John, who managed to secure it in place.

'Right.' Mackenzie dug out a small penlight and checked Stan's pupils. 'Sluggish. Indicative of concussion.'

John continued to check Stan's body for further injuries. 'Laceration to right thigh. Thankfully, he doesn't appear to have nicked the femoral artery but the bone doesn't look good either.'

'Agreed.'

'Hold this pad for me while I cut away the material around his thigh.'

'Any other injuries?' Mackenzie pressed one hand firmly to the pad and ran her other hand expertly over the rest of Stan's limbs. 'Right arm doesn't feel as it should.' She pressed her fingers to the radial pulse.

'Suspected fracture?' he asked after a moment.

'Probably to the humerus and wrist. The pulse point is faint.'

'OK. Let's get this leg stabilised.' They worked together, applying a tourniquet and bandage as well as splinting Stan's legs together for stability.

Once they were done, Mackenzie tucked the space blanket around Stan's legs then hooked the stethoscope into her ears and listened to Stan's chest again. 'Airways still clear but as the sun's now down, with chances of rain forecast, I'd really like to get him out of here as soon as possible.'

'Agreed.' They checked Stan's vital signs once more, determined to get him as stable as possible before transferring him to the stretcher.

'Stan?' Mackenzie called again, hoping for a response. 'Stan?'

'All in all, he's been very lucky,' John murmured. 'It could have been much worse.'

'Poor Anna,' she whispered.

'Anna?' The soft, barely audible word came from Stan's lips and Mackenzie immediately leaned closer.

'Stan? Can you hear me? It's Mackenzie.'

'Mac…?' Stan was starting to regain consciousness and the first thing he did was try to raise his hand to his head. John quickly held his arm still.

'You've had an accident, mate.' His tone was kind but firm. 'Stay still.'

'Accident? Where am I?'

'You're in the national park,' Mackenzie volunteered, but she looked at John. 'Do you remember what happened?'

'What?' Stan was clearly disoriented and as he had a probable concussion, there could well be amnesia to go along with it.

'Rest now. We're getting ready to evacuate you,' John said, as Mackenzie prepared the pain relief. He called down to Gordon, who was on the walkie-talkie to Ted, organising for the stretcher to be sent down.

The next half an hour was spent transferring Stan to the stretcher, clipping him in and having him winched to the top of the cliff. Once there, Bergan and Katrina took over Stan's medical care while Mackenzie was hooked into the winch and lifted to the top. John came after her and finally Gordon was up, too.

'A successful retrieval,' Ted announced, giving ranger Gordon a high-five.

'Let's get him back to the ambulance,' Bergan announced and with the paramedics they began the long trek back to where the ambulance was waiting. Now that the retrieval was over and done with, Mackenzie knew she should be feeling more calm and relaxed but because she still had to operate on Stan, her nerves were still taut.

Both she and John accompanied Stan in the back of the ambulance and once they arrived at Sunshine General they took him directly to Radiology, where Anna and the boys were able to see Stan, and ascertain for themselves that although he was quite badly banged up, he was indeed going to be OK.

'Can I be in the theatre?' Anna asked Mackenzie.

'Do you think that's a good idea?' Mackenzie asked. 'It might be better if you stay with your boys.'

'Their uncle has just arrived and they're happy to stay out here with him. Please, Mackenzie. I won't be a part of the team. I'll just be at the side, watching. I promise I won't get in the way.'

'It's not that I'm worried about you getting in the way,' Mackenzie offered. 'I'm worried about *you*.'

'Oh, you're so sweet, Mackenzie.' Anna hugged her close. 'It is your call and I'll abide by your decision.' The theatre nurse looked across at where her husband was still having another round of X-rays taken.

Mackenzie looked across at John, who shrugged. 'Doesn't bother me,' he murmured.

'I guess it will help put your mind at rest,' Mackenzie added. 'OK. If you're sure this is what you want.'

Anna sighed with relief. 'It is. Thank you.'

'OK. I'm going off to scrub,' Mackenzie said, and headed out of Radiology, leaving Stan in John's capable hands.

'Focused?' John asked a while later as he joined her at the scrub sink.

'Yes.' She glanced up at him and was surprised to find him smiling brightly at her. 'What?' She wished he wouldn't smile like that right now because just the sight of his gorgeous blue eyes twinkling at her caused her heart to skip a beat.

'You're brilliant,' he whispered, and before she knew which way was up, he'd leaned down and brushed a tantalising kiss across her lips.

'Don't do that,' she growled, and elbowed off the taps.

'Sorry.'

'You've ruined my focus.'

Instead of looking contrite, his grin widened. 'Sorry.'

'You don't look sorry.'

He shrugged a shoulder but after a moment his eyes sobered as he looked down at her. 'Let me know if things get too tough and I'll take over. It's always difficult to operate when the patient is someone you know.'

There was something in his tone that made her wonder if he hadn't had to endure a situation much the same as this, operating on someone he not only knew but loved. She swallowed, the next group of words leaving her lips before she could stop them. 'Did you have to operate on…?'

'My wife?' he finished. 'Yes. She had a punctured lung and I was trying to help in any way I could.' With that, John elbowed off the taps and turned away from her.

She hadn't meant to upset him, especially as they both needed their wits about them before heading into Theatre. She knew he was reticent about discussing his wife and daughter but she was positive he'd locked his inner self away for far too long, preferring to ignore the emotions of loss rather than dealing with them.

She knew all about that, thanks to her foster-system motto—the only person you could fully trust was yourself—but over the years and with the help of people like Bergan she'd started to realise it was possible to trust others. Perhaps it was up to her to help John take that giant step out of the past into the future…and hopefully it would be a future with her and Ruthie in it.

Mackenzie and John worked efficiently to fix Stan's fractured femur with an intramedullary Grosse and Kempf nail before adding a few plates and screws to the comminuted fracture of the right arm. While Mackenzie was conscious of Anna's presence behind her, the nurse kept her word and stayed out of the way, not making a peep.

'Thank you,' Anna said once Stan had been wheeled to Recovery. Mackenzie de-gowned before receiving a big hug from her friend.

'Go and drive the nurses in Recovery insane with your over-protective nurse-wife act.'

Anna smiled for the first time since they'd arrived at the hospital with Stan, and John watched the stress being replaced with relief as she hugged her friend again. 'Thanks, Mackenzie.' Anna looked over at him. 'And you, too, John. You have no idea…words… I can't express just how grateful I am.'

'We look after our own,' Mackenzie stated, before ushering her friend out the door, then turned to face John and breathed her own sigh of relief. 'I'm glad that's over.'

'You handled it all very well.'

'Trained to switch off emotions and click into professional mode,' she said, tapping the side of her head. 'I think I've been like that for most of my life.' Mackenzie headed into the anteroom to write up the notes and John followed. 'We're conditioned from a young age to hide our emotions, not be vulnerable.' She shook her head. 'It's sad.'

'But necessary,' John added.

'Perhaps in some instances but I don't want Ruthie to grow up feeling like that. I want her to feel loved and secure and valuable, not only to me but to whomever she may one day marry. I want her to be a confident teenager, able to say no to alcohol and drugs because she doesn't need them to fill the void in her life. I want her to keep talking to me, to be sharing her thoughts and dreams with me. I don't want her to hide her emotions, to ignore me or them because that only makes things ten times worse.'

She looked up at John, pen in hand, Stan's casenotes in front of her. 'Wasn't that how you felt about Mune-hie?

Wanting her to grow up to be an emotionally and mentally strong young woman?'

He stared at her for a long moment and when it didn't seem like he was going to answer Mackenzie sighed and turned her attention to writing up Stan's notes, a little disappointed that he hadn't immediately opened up and decided to share with her. She had to realise that although he'd shared one or two things with her about his family, that didn't mean he was ready to crack open like a piñata.

Once she'd finished the notes, she took off her gumboots and slipped on her clogs then picked up the notes. 'I'd better get these to Recovery.' It was as she headed for the door, conscious of the fact that John had stood there the entire time, silently watching her, that he finally spoke.

'It's not that easy for me, Mackenzie.' His words halted her and she turned back to look at him. 'Talking about them. I want to. I really do but...' He shrugged then crossed to her side and took her free hand in his. 'I'll try harder.'

'Why?'

'Why what?'

'Why do you want to try harder, John? You either want to open up to me or you don't. You either want whatever it is that exists between us to grow or you don't.' She let out a heavy sigh and slowly shook her head before meeting his gaze. 'I like you, John,' she said softly. 'A lot. I've hardly dated at all in the past five years, only every now and then when I couldn't stop Reggie from setting me up with someone.'

She shook her head and sighed. 'Look.' She gave his hand a little squeeze. 'For the first time in my life I can accept that there's something very real, very different from anything else I've ever felt going on between us. It's fresh and unique and incredibly scary but if you're not ready then you're not ready and I refuse to rush you.'

A small smile touched his lips. 'You've always been forthright and strong. It's one of the things I like most about you.'

'Thank you, John. That does mean a lot but at the moment I think it's probably better if we just take a step back, give each other some breathing space and then, if you feel you're ready—'

'It's not that I *don't* want to talk about them, Mackenzie,' John interrupted. 'I *do* want to share with you, about what our life was like, about our dreams and hopes for our daughter, but even just talking about the plans I had for Mune-hie's life brings back all the pain of losing her, knowing those plans will never, ever come to fruition.'

Mackenzie nodded. 'I get that, John, I really do, but *facing* your grief, letting out the pain you feel is the only way to bring healing. Have you ever allowed yourself to grieve for them? Or did you just feel you had to remain strong and sure of yourself in order to survive? To show yourself that while you were strong when they were alive, you could be equally as strong without them? That to grieve for their loss might mean you were weak?'

'Or that I might fall into the darkest of pits and never get out,' he growled, letting go of her hand. He shook his head and she could see his repressed anger and annoyance at her words. Mackenzie nodded. Anger was good. Anger was a breakthrough.

'You need to go into that pit, John. You need to face their loss. You need to really grieve for them.'

He glared at her and spread his arms wide. 'And what if I can't get out of the pit?' The words were that of a man on the brink of despair but he was still able to hold himself in check.

Mackenzie's heart pounded wildly against her ribs, seeing the anguish of his loss reflected in his eyes. She knew that pain, she knew that anguish and when she'd had to face it, she'd had John's firm arms around her shoulders, literally giving her a shoulder to cry on.

She took a step towards him and rested her hand on his cheek. She smiled up at him. 'You *will* get out of the pit, John. I promise you.'

'How? How can you promise that?'

'Because you'll be tethered to a rope and I'll be on the other end, hauling you back to the surface. Me and Ruthie and Bergan and the Allingtons and Anna and no doubt Stan, too. You're starting to surround yourself with people who genuinely care about you, and I'd also hazard a guess that there are plenty of other people you've worked with over the years who would also support you in any way they could, not to mention all your sisters and nieces and nephews as well.'

She stood on tiptoe and brushed a soft, friendly kiss across his cheek. 'You're not alone, John. Not any more. You were there when I needed you most. You were the one tethered to the other end of the rope while I descended into the pits of darkness and you gave me the strength and confidence I needed to get myself out.'

'But I was only with you for—'

'It doesn't matter how long we were together back then, or that you handed the rope over to Bergan, which was, in hindsight, the right thing to do. I think if you had stayed in my life I would have become far too dependent on you and at that time it was the last thing I needed.'

She smiled at him as she dropped her hand. 'You were my knight in shining armour and I can never thank you enough but what I can do is most definitely return the favour. I've told you I'm here for you, John, and I mean that, not only in the bonds of friendship but also in the bonds of a potential relationship. I'm a girl who's looking for permanence, for commitment, for as long as we both shall live.'

She took a step back, knowing she was probably saying too much but seemingly unable to stop herself. 'I'm not trying to scare you or pressure you. I'm trying to be open and honest with you.'

She tapped the casenotes. 'I'll deliver these and check on Stan.' She turned and headed to the door. 'Let me know when you're ready,' she said over her shoulder, and left the room.

John watched her go, unable to stop himself from checking out the gentle sway of her hips. Even in theatre scrubs she looked sexy. Darn, the woman was completely getting under his skin and in the rule of life as written and edited by John Watson, that was a no-no. However, what she'd said had made complete sense and he was beginning to realise, having seen the way she'd forged ahead with her own life, that he was probably already halfway down that dark pit and hadn't even realised it.

He closed his eyes and clenched his hands tight, imagining himself completely in the dark, holding onto a rope, and when he looked up at the speck of light above him, he saw Mackenzie's beautiful face smiling back down at him.

He was becoming far too attached to her, far too quickly. It wasn't right for him to move on with his life when Jacqueline and Mune-hie couldn't move on with theirs. His heart had been torn into pieces when he'd been unable to save them, unable to use all the skill and medical knowledge and supplies to save their lives.

He'd sat there and watched them die, watched the life slip from them, and at the same time it had slipped from him, too. For so long he'd wished he'd died along with them, that the three of them could at least have stayed together, but that hadn't been the case.

He knew Mackenzie had her own issues to face and deal with but she did it in her own way and he needed to do it in his. Yes, he'd told her he wanted to talk to her about his family and, yes, he appreciated her support but he wasn't ready. He knew he just wasn't ready. Throw into the mix the fact that he couldn't stop thinking about Mackenzie, wanting to hold her, kiss her, be with her, and he was adding a hefty helping of guilt to his already over-burdened conscience.

John quickly opened his eyes and shook his head. Too much. It was too much to process, to think about. His past was *his* past and that's where it was going to stay. He needed to cool things down with Mackenzie, put a bit of distance between them so he could figure out what to do next.

He squared his shoulders and with firm and determined strides he headed to the changing rooms, mentally closing the box that led to the pit. No. He was stronger without the need to relive his past. He could cope. He would continue on the path he'd always been on.

This was who he was and Mackenzie could either accept it or ignore it. Her choice.

CHAPTER TWELVE

BY THE TIME Mackenzie was ready to go home, pleased that Stan was now stable and surrounded by his loving family, she couldn't find John anywhere.

'I did see him talking to Leyton earlier,' Bergan told her when Mackenzie went to check the A and E department.

'What's Leyton doing here at this hour?' Mackenzie asked, knowing the hospital's chief executive officer usually kept strictly to office hours and it was now almost midnight.

'I don't know. Look, perhaps John had to leave.'

Mackenzie shook her head. 'He would have left me a message.'

'Well, I'll be heading home in another half an hour if you need a lift,' Bergan offered.

Mackenzie frowned, starting to wonder if John had indeed perhaps left the hospital without telling her. She had pushed him before and perhaps she'd pushed him a little too far this time. He'd told her he was happy to talk about his family but maybe that only meant on his own terms, when he was ready, not to have her just blurting out questions at odd moments.

She stood by what she'd said, though. Even during medical school during their psychology lessons they'd learnt about the different stages of grief and that it was better to deal with it than to bottle it up. John's roaming lifestyle, six months here, a year there, never really setting down roots, never really opening himself up to anyone, was no way to live a normal, healthy life. *He* was the one who had helped *her* to realise that so why couldn't he realise it for himself?

She thanked Bergan for the offer and headed back to John's office in the orthopaedic department, wondering if their paths had crossed. Mackenzie smiled and breathed a sigh of relief when she saw John sitting at his desk, filling in some paperwork.

'Hi. I've been trying to find you.'

John looked up and for a moment Mackenzie felt as though he was looking straight through her. There was no welcoming smile on his face and she felt a trickle of apprehension flood down her spine, her feminine intuition telling her that something was definitely wrong.

'Something wrong?' he asked, his tone light and even, not displaying any emotion at all.

'No, nothing is wrong. Stan's doing nicely and is about to be transferred to ICU. Anna is, understandably, much calmer and has arranged for her boys to go home with their uncle so she can nurse Stan through the night.'

'Good. Good.' He only glanced up once from what he was writing and as she came a little closer to his desk she realised he was filling in a registration form for the orthopaedic conference due to take place in Sydney the following week. Two of her colleagues had been planning to go, which meant they'd be light on staff during clinics, and if John was going, too, it would mean even longer hours for her. 'Heading to the conference?' she queried.

'Yes. Leyton requested I attend and present a paper.'

'Oh?'

'So I need to get this filled in now, scanned, copied

and emailed off to the relevant people so that funding and locums, etcetera, can start to be organised first thing tomorrow. Then I need to find my research from last year, when I was in Bangledesh for six months, reorganise the abstract and submit it to the conference committee as they've had two presenting surgeons pull out at the last minute.'

'OK.' She was quiet for a moment, trying to figure out what had happened to make him change. Was it just that he was busy? She knew that attending a conference wasn't as easy as just packing a bag and going, especially when the hospital was paying, as there was so much red tape involved.

Or was it something else? She couldn't help the thought that it was something she had done as his attitude towards her seemed very closed off.

She stood there for a few more minutes, just watching him write, unsure what to do next. She hated uncertainty, wishing that if John had an issue with her he'd just come right out and tell her what it was.

'Well...' She clasped her hands together in front of her. 'I'll organise another way of getting home.' With that, she turned on her heel and headed towards the door.

John put his pen down, closed his eyes for a moment, rubbing one hand over his forehead before he stood, calling her name. 'Mackenzie, wait.' He came round his desk but didn't come any further. She reached the door and turned to face him. 'I'd forgotten that we'd come in the same car. I do apologise.'

'It's all right. It's been a busy night. I need to go and collect Ruthie.'

'You wouldn't just let her sleep the rest of the night at the Allingtons?'

'Of course not. She *is* my daughter and it's hardly fair

on them to be woken up at the crack of dawn by an over-bright five-year-old. Honestly, from the moment she wakes up, she's "on". The questions start, so do the laughter and the smiles, and I could do with a bit of laughter and smiles in about five and a half hours' time.'

He shook his head in amazement. 'You're a good mother, Mackenzie.'

She shrugged one shoulder. 'I do the best I can.' She was still a little annoyed with him for the way he'd all but ignored her when she'd walked into his office and right now she just wanted to leave. 'Anyway, carry on with your paperwork. I'll see you…when I see you.'

She turned again and had taken a few steps down the department corridor before he called her name again. 'I'm sorry, Mackenzie. I thought I could do…this.' She hadn't turned round and part of him didn't blame her. He'd been rude to her just now but perhaps putting a bit of distance between them was the best thing to do.

'It's fine, John.' She took another step away from him, unable to turn and look at him.

'Mackenzie, wait.'

'Leave it, John.' She sighed then looked at him over her shoulder. 'I thought…I'd hoped we were on the same page.'

'We are, at least on some level.'

'That's not enough. I've been in a relationship that was one-sided before, that was filled with lies and unfaithfulness and passive-aggressive tendencies where Warick would make me feel that everything was always my fault.' She turned round, looking at him and shaking her head. 'I don't *need* to be in a relationship, John. I was doing just fine before you came here.'

'And yet you've confessed to dreaming about me,' he pointed out.

'That's right, and that's all they appear to be. Just dreams.

Dreams can't hurt me. Dreams are a figment of my imagination, of a world where I have a man who adores me, who cherishes me, who is addicted to loving me.' She impatiently blinked back the tears that were gathering behind her eyes. Now was not the time for her to turn into a blubbering mess.

'I truly believe what I said to you earlier. I don't think you've dealt with the deaths of your family and perhaps, until you do, we should simply remain as colleagues and neighbours.'

'And friends?'

'If you need me, John, I promise to be there for you.'

'To repay your debt? To help me as I helped you?' There was a hint of confusion in his voice, as though he still had no real idea why she was offering her help.

Mackenzie laughed without humour and raised her eyes heavenwards. 'Good Lord, for a man who is so intelligent, you really are thick.' She met his gaze and sighed, trying to figure out how best to get through to him.

'Of course you've had a big impact on my life and I'll thank you again and again for being strong when I was weak, but I've repaid you for that kindness by getting on with my life, for believing in the strength that you said you saw in me.

'I see that same strength in you, John, the strength to face your past, but right now you're too focused on plugging up the cracks I've made in your protective wall and I understand that, I really do. But there is absolutely no hope for anything real or permanent or life-changing to happen between us until you've come out from behind the fortress you've built around your heart.'

She watched as he shoved his hands into the pockets of his jeans, showing her he still needed to hide from the situation. 'I'm attracted to you and I know you're attracted to me. I'm not like other women you may have been involved with over the years because I genuinely care about you and I want you to find the peace that's been missing from your life, that you've been running from, for these past eight years.' Swiping a hand across her cheek to catch a stray tear sliding down her cheek, she gave him a watery smile. 'See you around, Dr Watson.'

With that, she resumed her way down the corridor, wishing that he'd call her back one last time, that he'd close the distance between them, that he'd gather her close in his arms and press his mouth to hers, telling her he was ready, ready to let go of the past and to move forward with her by his side.

But he didn't do any of that and this time, as the tears gathered in her eyes, she let them fall.

'Ruthie keeps asking for him,' Mackenzie told her friends as they crowded around the small table in the coffee shop. Sunainah and Reggie had just finished their shifts and Bergan and Mackenzie were about to start theirs. She'd dropped Ruthie off at school and come straight here, desperate for her friends to cheer her up.

'How have things been between the two of you at work?' Sunainah asked as she cut into her pancakes.

'Strained. We only talk to each other when absolutely necessary and even then it's mostly about patients. Thankfully, he's been away at the conference for the past few days, which has given me a bit of a breather, but he gets back tomorrow.'

'Isn't that your day off?'

She nodded. 'I swapped with Sonny. Saturday is Ruthie day and after a quick ward round in the morning I'm going to spend the day with my girl, but after that I have no doubt the avoidance dance between John and myself will start again.' She shook her head. 'I knew I shouldn't have moved so fast but I...' She stopped.

'You couldn't help it,' Bergan said softly, placing a reassuring hand on Mackenzie's shoulder. 'He's the first man I've ever seen turn your head so fast.'

'And now Ruthie's attached to him and is missing him and I just should have been more careful.'

'Will you stop beating yourself up?' Reggie said, her bright and cheery smile providing support for Mackenzie. 'Things will work out. I just know it.'

'I'm glad you do,' Mackenzie mumbled as she poked at her scrambled eggs, her appetite having vanished. 'I rely on you for my healthy dose of optimism, Reggie, because right now I don't foresee a happy ending for us.'

'Do you know what you need?' Reggie continued.

'A brain scan?'

Sunainah and Bergan laughed but Mackenzie just placed her fork on her plate and buried her face in her hands.

'What do I need, Reggie?'

'A day out. I have the day off tomorrow, too, so why don't I meet you and Ruthie at the wildlife park?'

'Yes. Good idea,' Sunainah agreed. 'You know how Ruthie loves that place and it always relaxes you.'

Mackenzie instantly baulked at the idea. The wildlife park was now also filled with wonderful memories of the time she'd spent there with John but if she was serious about getting on with her life, she had to turn and face the pain. Besides, it wouldn't be fair to Ruthie to deny her the outing.

She lowered her hands and looked at her three best friends. They'd always been there for her, helping her through both little and big things. Who had been there for John? True, he was the one who had shut himself off and chances are his older sisters probably had no idea just how much of his life he'd locked away from others. He'd had no one there, day in, day out, helping him to smile, helping him to step into the sunshine and live again.

'What do you say?' Reggie continued.

Mackenzie nodded and smiled warmly at her friends. 'I think that idea sounds like a beauty.'

Later that day, after she'd managed to finish clinic a little earlier than expected, she went round to Grandma Liz's to collect Ruthie, unable to keep the excitement out of her voice as she told her daughter of their plans for the following day.

'And John can come, too,' Ruthie told her. 'He loved it last time and—'

'John will be working tomorrow.' Mackenzie cut her off. 'Sorry, sweetheart. But Reggie's going to meet us there.'

'Oh.' Ruthie gave a big sigh. 'I haven't seen John for ages and ages.'

'He's been away at a conference,' Mackenzie said as they pulled into the cul-de-sac.

'There he is!' Ruthie's excited squeal penetrated Mackenzie's ears and the instant she'd brought the small car to a stop Ruthie had unclipped her seatbelt and was scrambling over the front seat of the car, opening the door and racing out towards John before Mackenzie could stop her.

'John! John!' she heard the little girl calling excitedly as John carried a duffel bag from his car towards his townhouse. Mackenzie went after her, watching as John turned to face her. He dropped his duffel bag and held out his arms wide, collecting Ruthie up and into his arms before spinning her round and holding her close.

A lump immediately formed in her throat at the sight they made, like a father and daughter reunited after a long time. The look on John's face as he closed his eyes and breathed in Ruthie's effervescence was one of sheer joy. Mackenzie's step faltered as she watched them, wishing and hoping that he would willingly break down his barriers and let them both in. Somewhere, somehow, when she hadn't even realised it, this man had crept into her life and stolen her heart. Now it seemed he was intent on breaking it as well.

She hadn't been able to tell any of her friends, not even Bergan, just how much she'd missed John these past couple of weeks. How she'd lain awake at night, forcing herself not to go over every touch, every nuance, every look, and failing miserably. How she'd woken either from thrilling dreams about him or with tears already on her cheeks. It had been easier this past week simply because he hadn't been right in front of her, reminding her of how much she'd once again lost. He really was so near yet so far.

She stood nearby, as though restricted from going any closer to him by an invisible barrier. Ruthie was chattering away in her usual animated manner, seated comfortably in the strong circle of his arms as he listened intently to what she was saying, nodding and murmuring in the right parts. Finally, Ruthie paused for breath and John looked her way.

'Hi.'

'Hi.' She watched as his smile remained fixed in place, changing from one of openness with Ruthie to a slightly guarded one with her. 'How was the conference?'

He shrugged one shoulder. 'OK.' Silence seemed to stretch between them and even though Ruthie was back to chattering away, the uncomfortable undercurrent intensified.

'And tomorrow we're going to the wildlife park again,' the little girl told him with evident excitement. 'And Reggie's going to meet us there but Mummy said you couldn't come because you had to work and I was really sad because I want you to come more than anything and then I saw you here and then I was really happy because I've missed you so much, John.'

With that, she buried her face in his neck once more. John placed a protective hand on Ruthie's head and Mackenzie could clearly see the attachment he had to her daughter.

The lump in her throat intensified as she knew exactly how Ruthie felt and she bit her lip to try and keep her emotions in check. She'd missed John, too and of course she wanted him to go to the wildlife park with them tomorrow but John had chosen to keep his heart locked safely away and there was nothing she could do about it. What she *did* have to do was to find a way to dissociate Ruthie from being so dependent upon John.

'Well—' She started to speak, astonished when her voice came out all squeaky. She cleared her throat and tried again. 'Well, we'd better go. We're already running behind our night-time schedule.'

'No!' Ruthie clung tighter to John.

'Come on, Ruthie,' Mackenzie pleaded, definitely not in the mood for one of her daughter's tantrums. 'It's time for a bath.'

'I don't want one.' If Ruthie had been standing on the ground Mackenzie was sure she would have stamped her foot. She racked her tired, sluggish mind, trying to think of things to sweeten the pot in order to gain her daughter's co-operation.

'You can sleep in my bed with me tonight.' Mackenzie dangled the carrot and John looked at Ruthie and nodded.

'That sounds good.'

'You stay, too, John.'

Both adults instantly looked at each other, their eyes

widening. A flood of pictures flashed through Mackenzie's mind, all of them having definitely been a part of her
dreams at one time or another

'Uh...' John quickly shifted Ruthie in his arms and set
her back on the ground. 'Your mum is right, Ruthie. I do
have a lot of work to do so, uh...you head on home and I'll
see you later.' Even just the thought of stepping foot into
Mackenzie's place was enough to set John's blood pumping faster around his body.

During his time at the conference he'd felt more dis-
jointed than ever. He'd been surrounded by hundreds of
people, some he'd worked with over the years, others he'd
only just met for the first time. After his presentation he'd
been offered two different jobs, one of which was a trav-
elling Fellowship, something that ordinarily would have
appealed to him, but for some reason it now held no temp-
tation.

Unable to shake the discontent he hadn't expected, he'd
left the conference a day early and headed to the Blue
Mountains, where he'd enjoyed the solitude, going on a
long walk...one that had ended at the exact spot where he'd
first met Mackenzie. It was as though his subconscious
had taken him back to the place where it had all begun,
with him helping a brave woman to breathe through her
contractions.

As he'd stood there he'd placed his hand against the tree
and closed his eyes. There he'd seen Mackenzie's bright
and smiling face, her laughter, her sparkling eyes, her rosy
cheeks, her luscious lips, and for the first time in a long
time he was able to draw in a deep and cleansing breath.
Mackenzie. Thoughts of her had made him smile, made
him feel as though an enormous weight had been lifted
from him. 'Mackenzie.' He'd breathed her name and the
sound had been cleansing and filled with hope.

Then, not two minutes after he'd arrived home, he'd had
Ruthie hurtling towards him like she'd done to her mother
on the first day he'd met her. It had been the most natural
thing in the world to open his arms and scoop her up, and
the happiness and love he had for the child had bubbled
up through his heart and overflowed.

'Will you come to the wildlife park?' Ruthie was asking him rather impatiently, which obviously meant she'd
already asked him once and he'd been too busy thinking
about her gorgeous mother to listen.

'I can try,' he promised, his gaze briefly flicking to see
what Mackenzie thought of the idea. She shrugged one
shoulder as though it didn't really bother her. He hoped
it did because the last thing he wanted was for Mackenzie to become indifferent to him. Although he may have
had an epiphany of sorts up on the Blue Mountains, actually standing in front of her and confessing as much was
a completely different kettle of fish.

'OK, Ruthie. Let's go inside, please.'

With great reluctance and showing she wasn't at all
happy with having to leave *her* John, Ruthie ignored Mackenzie's proffered hand and turned and stomped off towards the house.

'Excuse my daughter's bad manners. She hasn't been
herself lately.'

'Is she all right? She's not sick?' The concern in his
voice was mirrored in his expression.

'She's fine, John.' Mackenzie was about to say more
but stopped and bit her tongue.

'But you just said—'

'It doesn't matter.' She turned and started walking towards her car.

'Mackenzie, if there's something wrong with her,
please, let me help.'

She turned back to face him. 'She misses you, John. She *really* misses you. She keeps asking me what she's done wrong because you don't talk to her any more.' Mackenzie couldn't help the surge of anger, frustration and pain that flooded through her. 'She's only five and she bonded with you the instant you met. She loves you, John.'

She sniffed and shook her head, looking up at the night sky rather than the look of regret evident in his big blue eyes. 'It's my fault. I shouldn't have let her get so attached. I'll deal with it. She won't bother you again.'

John stood there and watched, for the second time, as Mackenzie walked away from him. He knew he should go to her, grab her and kiss her and tell her that he'd been a complete idiot and now that he was more certain of his feelings for her, he never wanted to let either her or Ruthie go. He wanted to tell her that he'd missed them both…but he didn't.

The words were choking him and so instead he watched Mackenzie and Ruthie disappear into their town-house, away from his view.

Ruthie loved him? That was…amazing. Fantastic. Brilliant, because he loved her right back. But what about her mother? Had he been too closed off? Too stubborn? Was it too late?

As he went into his own cold and empty town-house, he dropped his duffel on the ground by the door and barely resisted putting his fist through the wall.

'You're an idiot,' he told himself briskly, because it hadn't been until the moment he'd seen her walk away tonight that he'd finally realised why he'd missed her so much.

He was in love with Mackenzie Fawles.

CHAPTER THIRTEEN

'Look, Reggie. *Look!*' Ruthie pulled Reggie over to look at the macaw, which was once again flying around the wildlife park. 'Last time, Reggie, I got to stroke it and it ate out of my hand and it really tickled.' She looked up at her mother, who immediately pasted on a smile. 'Didn't it, Mummy? It tickled.'

'So you said,' Mackenzie agreed.

'And John and Mummy took photos of me.' A little frown crinkled Ruthie's forehead. 'I wish John was here,' she stated, and once again looked at her mother as though wanting her to make John materialise from thin air. 'Why isn't he here, Mummy?'

Mackenzie glanced at Reggie, silently asking her what to do. Reggie smiled brightly and gave both her shoulders a big shrug, indicating that she really had no clue. They'd been there for the past three hours and everywhere they went Ruthie would tell Reggie what had happened the last time they'd come with John. Every time her daughter mentioned his name, it felt as though a knife was being turned deep within Mackenzie's heart.

'Ooh, look at that,' Reggie said, pointing to a pelican that had flown gracefully over to the large lake, performing a perfect and smooth landing.

'Ooh, yes.' Ruthie clapped her hands, successfully diverted once more. In fact, Mackenzie was sure she'd spent much of her time trying her best to divert Ruthie's attention to different things in order to get her to stop talking about John.

Mackenzie didn't want to know about John, didn't want to think about John, didn't want to—

'Hello,' a deep baritone voice, one that had the ability to send her entire body into overdrive, said right behind her. Mackenzie instantly spun round, feeling as though she was hallucinating as she saw John standing there, dressed casually in jeans and navy-blue polo shirt, a wide smile on his face.

'John!' She was too shocked to process that he was really there but he was. He was there. He'd promised Ruthie he'd try to make it and he had but…why? If he'd decided not to have anything to do with them, she wished he'd just keep his distance. That way, she at least had some hope to try and find some way of healing her heart.

Before she could say another word, Ruthie spied John and came running over to him. 'John. John. John!' He scooped her up and she wrapped her arms about him, snuggling her little head into his neck, a delighted smile on her face. 'You're here. I wished you could come and you did!' She lifted her head. 'Look, Mummy. Look, Reggie. John's here. John's here.' She wiggled in his arms, doing a little dance.

'So I see,' Mackenzie said, pulling her light cardigan across her body, even though she wasn't cold.

'And the macaw's out again, John.'

'I know.' He grinned at Ruthie, seeming very relaxed and at ease. Mackenzie swallowed as hope began to rise within her. Was it possible? Could she take it as read that his presence here meant that…? She stopped her thoughts, knowing she was probably getting ahead of herself once more.

'And the pelican just did a big skidding landing in the water.' Ruthie pointed with excitement down towards the lake. 'Come on, John. Let's go look at it.'

John pressed a kiss to Ruthie's cheek before putting her down. 'I'll be there really soon,' he said, 'but first I just need to talk to your mummy.'

'But, John.' Ruthie frowned at him and put her hands on her hips.

'I feel like ice cream,' Reggie said from behind them all. 'Come on, Ruthie, let's go get an ice cream for everyone and then we can come back and all go down to the lake together.'

'Ice cream!' Once more diverted, Ruthie's smile was back as she slipped her hand into Reggie's. Mackenzie shot her friend a grateful look before the two of them headed over the kiosk.

'I must remember to thank Reggie later,' John remarked as he immediately took Mackenzie's hand in his and led her over to a shady gum tree.

'John? What—?' Still rather annoyed at the way his arrival had not only knocked all rational thought from her mind but had somehow caused her heart to go into palpitations, Mackenzie tried to withdraw her hand from his. He didn't let her, not until they were both seated on a soft cushion of grass.

'Sorry. I know I'm being high-handed but I hope you'll forgive me.'

'Forgive you? For what?'

'For being a complete and utter idiot.'

'Oh?'

'Mackenzie…you were right. I've locked my heart away, I haven't dealt with my grief, and the truth of the matter…'

He stopped and exhaled slowly, and it was then she started to see not only how nervous he appeared but how difficult it was for him to be this open with her. Still, she held her tongue, knowing it was important for him to do this. He looked down at his hands, then carefully reached out and took hers in his again.

'The truth is…I don't know how to. I don't know how to deal with it.' He raised his gaze to hers and she saw a man who was completely unguarded, raw and vulnerable.

'I can't do this on my own. I don't want to do this on my own but you're right. If I want to move forward, to move on with my life, to not live the rest of my life as a robotic nomad then I need…I need to face losing them.'

Mackenzie couldn't help the tears that pricked behind her eyes at his words. 'Oh, John. Of course I'll help you. I'd do anything for you. *Anything.*'

'Because you owe me a debt?'

'No.' Her smile was wobbly and she rolled her eyes before giving his hand a little squeeze. 'Because I'm in love with you.'

John stared at her for a moment before exhaling a long and slow breath. 'I thought I'd ruined everything with my stupid stubbornness.'

She shook her head and lifted his hand to her lips, and John knew he really didn't deserve such attention from her, but if it was offered, he was going to take it. Mackenzie loved him. She loved him! His heart soared with this news but he knew if they were going to move forward into the future together he needed to be more open about his past.

'I want to tell you about Jacqueline and Mune-hie.'

'John, we don't have to star—'

'Yes. Yes, we do have to start right now because I've already wasted too much time and I want the next phase of my life to begin right this second, with you by my side knowing about my family.'

Mackenzie knew it wasn't easy for him to share in such a way and seeing the determination in his eyes made her heart burst with love for him. She waited as patiently as she could, not wanting to rush him, and after taking a few long breaths and gathering his thoughts he looked deeply into her eyes.

'We'd returned to Tarparnii for a quick visit. We took Mune-hie back several times a year, knowing it was important for her to understand her heritage, but while we were there...' He stopped. 'The village she came from was a very small one, no more than three huts with about thirty people living there, all of them suffering from malnutrition or disease or...'

He exhaled sharply and she could see the sadness in his eyes as he remembered. 'When we arrived, we didn't realise half the village were extremely sick. I managed to radio for back-up support from some of my Pacific Medical Aid buddies who I'd worked with over the years, but by the time they arrived, two days later, twenty of the thirty people had died.'

'Oh, John.' Mackenzie raised her free hand to her mouth, her lips trembling as she slowly shook her head from side to side. 'How utterly devastating.'

'It was. It turned out to be something like influenza. It's called *yellom cigru fever* and a very bad strain had hit the village. Usually, it's only native Tarparniians who are affected but Jacqueline was always very fragile. She'd survived ovarian cancer but the chemotherapy had made her sick for a long, long time. Her immune system was low and she became infected, too. She suffered a punctured lung and I managed to install a drain to remove the fluid from the pleural cavity but I only had a first-aid kit and the medical supplies were in short supply—'

Mackenzie reached forward and placed her fingers on his lips. 'Stop. Don't.' She shook her head, tears rolling down her cheeks. 'You don't need to—'

He clutched at her hand and squeezed it tight, tears in his own eyes as he looked into Mackenzie's. 'I couldn't save her.'

'John. Oh, John.' Mackenzie could take it no longer and gathered him close into her arms. He held onto her tightly, needing her support, her arms around him. 'It was so quick. First Mune-hie, then Jacqueline.' The words were mumbled against her shoulder and she eased back to look at him.

'I am so sorry for your loss, John.' She touched her mouth to his, wanting to offer him healing and love and a belief that he'd made the right decision in opening up to her. 'Truly. What you must have gone through. No wonder you wanted to bottle it up.'

'But it was time.' He eased back and shifted round to lean against the trunk of the large eucalypt, drawing Mackenzie close into the circle of his arms. 'It was time for me to let go. To move forward.' He shook his head. 'Going to the conference and being alone in an impersonal hotel room again made me realise just how empty my life had become, how I've spent too long pushing people away.'

'It's easy to do and unless you have someone grounding you—'

'Or holding onto the rope?' He smiled.

'Keeping you tethered,' she hiccuped, returning his smile. 'It isn't easy.'

'I left the conference early.' His confession caused her eyebrows to rise in surprise. 'I delivered my paper then high-tailed it out of there. I felt so closed in with nowhere to go so I headed up to the Blue Mountains and went for a hike.'

'Finding beauty in nature,' she remarked, waving her hand around at the picturesque landscape presently before them.

'I went back to the tree where we first met.'

'Really? I didn't think you were that sentimental.'

'Neither did I. I put my hand on that tree trunk and I felt as though I was linked back to you, to Ruthie, to the life I was starting to build here. I want to keep building that life, Mackenzie. I want to build it with *you*.'

He stared into her eyes. 'You have brought such happiness and sunshine into my life and I don't ever want to let it go. Moving forward, with you, is the only way for me and I'm sorry, so very sorry, if I've caused you any pain over the past weeks.' He raised his eyebrows, giving her a pleading look. 'Forgive me?'

'Of course.' Mackenzie pressed her lips to his as though to prove to him that she meant it. 'I love you, John Watson. There's nothing you can do to change that and together we'll be happy and spread our own brand of sunshine, showering Ruthie and our friends with love and support.'

Neither of them spoke for a few seconds as John kissed her, this woman who was so incredibly wonderful. There was one other thing he needed to clear up, though, to make absolutely sure they were on the same page. He pulled back and looked down into her smiling face. 'Also, Mackenzie, we perhaps need to discuss…children.' He swallowed over the question.

Her eyes widened in surprise. 'Do *you* want to have more children?'

John nodded then glanced past her to where he could see Ruthie and Reggie heading in their direction, Ruthie's ice cream beginning to melt everywhere.

'Ruthie has helped to heal that part of my life, to let me see that I *am* capable of opening my heart to love a child again.' He smiled, quite bemused as Ruthie and Reggie drew closer. 'I used to think it was OK to be Mr Independent, to not need anyone, because isn't that what independence means?' He shook his head as though discounting his own question.

'You and Ruthie have shown me that the more I can open up to you, the more vulnerable I make myself to those who love me and, therefore, I'll become more open. I realised when I was in the Blue Mountains that although I hadn't given you and Ruthie permission to infiltrate my heart…you somehow managed to do it. I was being handed a second chance at happiness on a silver platter.'

He pressed his lips to hers before helping her to her feet. 'I'm grabbing my second chance because the happier *I* am, the more I can be of value to other people.'

Mackenzie stood beside him, her arms around his neck as she looked into his eyes. 'You *are* of value to me already, John.'

'Thank you.'

'Well, things seem to be coming up roses over here,' Reggie said, giving them a knowing wink, her smile bright as she handed Mackenzie and John an ice cream each.

'Why was you kissing Mummy?' Ruthie wanted to know.

'Er…' John looked at Mackenzie, who shrugged a shoulder. He returned his attention to Ruthie. 'Because…' He stopped and then surprised Mackenzie by kneeling down and whispering something in Ruthie's ear. As she watched, the smile on her daughter's face became big and bright, her eyes shining with excited delight.

'Now?' Ruthie asked.

'Very soon,' John confirmed as he stood up.

'Very soon what?' Mackenzie wanted to know.

'Ahh.' John tapped the side of his nose, indicating he had a secret. 'You'll find out soon enough, but first let's finish our ice creams.'

It must have been the fastest ice cream Mackenzie had ever eaten and she almost gave herself a headache. John took his time then offered to take Ruthie to the nearby tap so she could wash her hands, leaving Mackenzie alone with Reggie.

'Do I congratulate you?' Reggie asked, hugging her friend close.

'I don't know.' Mackenzie was still a little puzzled. John may have opened up to her, may have accepted her love and discussed a future together, but beyond that she still wasn't sure what it all meant.

'But you do love him?'

'Yes. Oh, yes.'

'And he knows that?'

'Yes.'

Reggie breathed a sigh of relief. 'Good.'

'Hey, Mummy!' Ruthie called to her, waving brightly, John still by her side. 'The macaw's over there again. Come on. I want to say hello to my friend.' And with that, she ran across the grassy area to where a crowd was already gathering near the brightly coloured bird and its trainer. John grinned widely and beckoned them over, falling behind to whisper something in Reggie's ear.

'Ooh!' Reggie squealed but quickly composed her face into her usual smile when Mackenzie turned round.

'What's going on?' she asked.

Reggie shrugged and linked arms with her. 'Let's get a good view of this macaw. I haven't seen it up close in ages.'

Mackenzie allowed herself to be led by her friend to the front of the group but then looked back for John and

Ruthie, finally spying them on the other side of the crowd, Ruthie safe and secure in John's arms. She relaxed a little as Reggie pulled out her camera, ready to get some shots.

'And today,' the ranger was saying, 'we have a very special treat that Marvin…' he stroked the macaw '…might be able to help us with. Now, can I have a volunteer, please?'

Many people put up their hands and, of course, Ruthie's was one of them. The ranger looked around at the eager faces then pointed to Ruthie. She smiled brightly and clapped wildly, and as she was still in John's arms, instead of putting her down, he carried her out to the front. The ranger asked their names and they supplied them for the gathered crowd.

Ruthie couldn't resist gently stroking Marvin again but this time, instead of getting the macaw to eat some food from Ruthie's hand, the parrot dipped his head into a special feed bag and came out with something round and shiny in his beak. He tilted his head towards Ruthie, who dutifully held out her hand nice and flat. Marvin dropped the shiny thing into Ruthie's hand and the little girl squealed with delight.

Reggie was madly taking photos and from their choice position in the front Mackenzie could clearly see what the shiny thing was. A stunningly beautiful solitaire diamond ring. Then John put Ruthie down and stepped forward, going down on bended knee in front of *her*. Some people in the crowd started clapping and whooping but the ranger held up his hands for silence.

'Mackenzie,' John said, and when he took her hand in his, she only then realised she was trembling. Her heart began to pound in double time as she looked from the shiny ring in her daughter's hands to the man before her. 'I am addicted to you and I hope you're equally as addicted to me because I need you, Mackenzie. Not only that, but…'

he placed his free hand over his heart, his gaze more intense than she'd ever seen before '…I *love* you. Most passionately. And I hope you'll consent to become my wife.'

He paused, waiting for her answer, but Mackenzie was just too stunned to speak, unable to believe just how happy she felt.

'Mummy!' Ruthie prompted in a loud whisper as she gave the ring to John. 'You're supposed to say "yes".'

'Oh…uh…of course.' Mackenzie smiled down at the man of her dreams, love shining brightly in her face. 'Yes. Yes, John.'

The crowd began to clap and cheer and whoop and after John had placed the ring on Mackenzie's finger, Reggie still taking photos of everything, he gathered Ruthie into his arms and stood between *his* girls.

'I love you,' he said again, softly, quietly, intimately.

'I love you, too,' she replied.

'And what about me?' Ruthie demanded, and both adults laughed, each placing a kiss on the little girl's cheeks.

'We love you the most!' they said in unison, all of them the happiest they'd ever been in their lives.

EPILOGUE

'IT'S YOUR WEDDING day! I can't believe one of us is finally getting married!' Reggie was jumping around in the small room of the church reserved for the bride to make last minute adjustments.

'You're worse than Ruthie,' Bergan said, as she smoothed a hand down her bridesmaid dress before turning to look at the bride. 'I cannot believe how stunning you look,' she said, giving her friend an air kiss. 'The beautiful, blushing bride.'

Mackenzie laughed, looking at her three best friends, all dressed in a dress of their own choosing because she wanted them to be as comfortable as possible on her wedding day. The dresses reflected their personalities. Bergan's sleek and sexy burgundy dress fitted her like a glove. Reggie had opted for a knee length pale pink tutu dress with loads of tule and lace, and Sunainah had chosen to wear a stunning sari of deep emerald.

Ruthie's dress, though, was the best as far as Mackenzie was concerned. She'd insisted on having the exact same wedding dress as her mother. 'So we can be twins,' she'd told her when they'd started discussing the wedding two months ago and so the dressmaker had been tasked to make two brides' dresses, one adult size and one for a growing five-and-a-half-year-old girl. The white raw satin with big medieval long sleeves and a flowing train fitted Mackenzie perfectly, her hair swirled into loose curls, piled onto her head with a lovely crown of flowers as a finishing touch. And Ruthie was her exact replica.

'I think John's going to like me the bestest,' Ruthie said, staring at her reflection in the mirror. 'Because I look like a fairy princess!'

Reggie had laughed, Sunainah joining in as they joined Ruthie in front of the mirror.

'What are we going to do with them?' Bergan asked rhetorically as she came to stand beside Mackenzie.

'I do not know.' Mackenzie turned to face her oldest friend. 'Bergan, I need to thank you.'

'No. No. Don't start.' Bergan held up her hand to stop her friend. 'We're all wearing make-up and if I start to cry, I'll have to do the whole thing again and we don't have time.'

Mackenzie breathed out, knowing what her friend had said was true but also needing to let her know just how much she loved her. 'I'm so glad we're friends.'

'I said, stop!' Bergan sniffed, her stern words belying the love Mackenzie could see reflected in her honey brown eyes. 'Yes I love you, too. Yes it's good we've been friends for such a long time and blah blah blah. Let's go get you married to that impatient man waiting at the front of the church.' Her words were brisk and matter-of-fact and as per usual, made Mackenzie laugh which was just what she needed right now.

'It might be your turn next,' Mackenzie said and Bergan's shout of laughter could no doubt be heard right throughout the church.

'You are funny, Kenz.'

'I do try.'

'Right.' Bergan clapped her hands and handed out floral bouquets so that when the wedding planner opened the door, they were all lined up and ready.

'The groom is beginning to get rather impatient,' the planner said and Mackenzie couldn't help but smile widely.

'He's waited a long time for this day,' she replied and as they started out of the room, Reggie leading the way, followed by Sunainah and then Begad, Mackenzie stayed at the back of the packed church and reached for her daughter's hand. 'Ready?'

Ruthie nodded. 'I'm really, really, really, really, really happy, Mummy.'

'Me, too,' Mackenzie laughed and together, they set off down the aisle to marry John.

* * * * *

A sneaky peek at next month…

Medical Romance™

CAPTIVATING MEDICAL DRAMA—WITH HEART

My wish list for next month's titles…

In stores from 7th June 2013:

☐ NYC Angels: Making the Surgeon Smile
— Lynne Marshall

& NYC Angels: An Explosive Reunion — Alison Roberts

☐ The Secret in His Heart — Caroline Anderson

& The ER's Newest Dad — Janice Lynn

☐ One Night She Would Never Forget — Amy Andrews

& When the Cameras Stop Rolling… — Connie Cox

Available at WHSmith, Tesco, Asda, Eason, Amazon and Apple

Just can't wait?

Visit us Online — You can buy our books online a month before they hit the shops! **www.millsandboon.co.uk**

0513/03

Special Offers

Every month we put together collections and longer reads written by your favourite authors.

Here are some of next month's highlights— and don't miss our fabulous discount online!

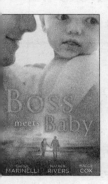

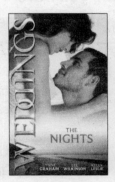

On sale 17th May   On sale 7th June   On sale 7th June

Save 20%
on all Special Releases

Find out more at
www.millsandboon.co.uk/specialreleases

*Visit us
Online*

The World of Mills & Boon®

There's a Mills & Boon® series that's perfect for you. We publish ten series and, with new titles every month, you never have to wait long for your favourite to come along.

Blaze.
Scorching hot, sexy reads
4 new stories every month

By Request
Relive the romance with the best of the best
9 new stories every month

Cherish™
Romance to melt the heart every time
12 new stories every month

Desire™
Passionate and dramatic love stories
8 new stories every month

Join the Mills & Boon Book Club

Want to read more **Medical** books?
We're offering you **2 more** absolutely **FREE!**

We'll also treat you to these fabulous extras:

- 🌹 **Exclusive offers and much more!**

- 🌹 **FREE home delivery**

- 🌹 **FREE books and gifts with our special rewards scheme**

Get your free books now!

visit www.millsandboon.co.uk/bookclub
or call Customer Relations on 020 8288 2888